JESSE NEO
THE MERGE
A psychological horror novel

THE
MERGE
A psychological horror novel

JESSE NEO

First paper edition, February 2026
Published by Neoxide Books

ISBN 978-1-7644867-0-5 (Paperback)

CONTENTS

For Joe, for introducing me to horror

CHAPTER 1
HUMILIATION

I swear I didn't mean to get caught, or parade my own humiliation. But in the end, it was my fault for being so arrogantly creative. That's why, when the dying language I was meant to preserve and extract findings from didn't reveal the results I intended—I made it all up.

Rows of chairs and long tables filled the room. The air could churn butter with the faint buzz of speakers along the walls. I could feel the heat of shame burning through my face, branding my name in the silence as I stood there unsure how to react. The shame mercilessly dug into me beneath the fluorescent lights of the conference room on level 13, 333 George Street, Sydney.

"So, you admit the entire research was fabricated?" said the panelist in the front row as she rose from her seat. The scrape of her chair cut through the tension. She leveled her pen at me like a sword.

The way she looked at me felt like a mortal challenge. It was a steady and deliberate accusation with justifiable merit. I could feel the cortisol surge through me, my body's silent alarm converting fear into heat, heat into itch, until my skin burned as if it were trying to escape itself.

She had introduced herself as Professor Caroline Stone of Western Sydney University. Her name was so revered in linguistics it functioned as its own credential. She was celebrated for her lifetime of work documenting and preserving Australia's Aboriginal languages.

In a way, her scorn reached farther than the conference hall and the small meeting rooms at the end. It didn't just bruise the editors and publishers gathered here at the International Conference on Linguistic Dynamics, but also rippled through the researchers, my own university, and the fragile architecture of my future—my graduation, tenure, survival. How far the damage would spread depended on how deep her connections ran.

Rows of faces blurred into a single mass of expectation. The steady tapping of keyboards faded, one keystroke at a time. Pens stilled, clattered once or twice, until everyone was in completely stunned silence. Every gaze in the room fixed on me like my life was in danger. It probably was, metaphorically, of course.

I stayed frozen beneath the harsh glare of the projector, my slide looming above like a sabotaging witness against me. I felt stripped bare, as if I was nothing more than a fragment of evidence laid out for examination.

Everywhere I looked, the light fractured. It bent, shimmered, and reshaped objects around me into things that shouldn't exist. It was on the phone screen beside my laptop, in the rows of empty glasses lining the sideboard at the far corner of the room, even in the metal of the elevators at the back. Each reflection held a fragment of someone's face that was half-stretched, half-still, caught between movement and memory.

When I caught my reflection in the side panel of the podium, the brass gleamed like liquid mercury. My own eyes stared back. And they were wide, uncertain, and hunted.

Alongside my face, a woman about my age met my gaze in the same reflection. At first, she seemed unremarkable with a conference badge and a notebook. There was the faint glint of what I thought were earbuds, but upon closer inspection, realized were hearing aids. She didn't flinch. Her lips were curved just enough to suggest a smile, though when I looked again, her face was still. Yet, I could feel her thoughts bleeding through the air: *he's finished. He'll never publish again.* Every whisper in the hallway already had my name in it.

Still in the reflection, a few seats away, a man—probably another PhD candidate—watched me through the sheen of his tablet. His face was angled just enough to catch the light. His hair looked like something preserved from the early 2000s. It was cut short at the sides, gelled into rigid peaks on top. His expression was unreadable, though the corners of his eyes tightened even as his mouth held a smile. For a moment, I thought he was filming me—archiving the fall of another fraud, feeding it to the digital mob of viral content. The light from his screen pulsed softly, and in one brief shimmer I could've sworn my lips were forming words I hadn't dared to speak aloud.

"I wouldn't say falsified," I said, trying my best to sound calm despite the lump forming in my throat. "I constructed a language. The purpose was to—"

"You *constructed* it?" Caroline repeated the word like it was a revolting curse.

The microphone caught the sharp exhale of someone's breath. A few soft yet nervous laughs slipped out. The rest shifted in their seats, hands idly aligning pens, eyes pretending to read the slides, doing anything to avoid looking at me.

I caught Jolin's face in the second row. She was dressed decades ahead of her age and for the current fashion trends. I never understood her fascination for metallic textures, asymmetrical folds, and light-reflective fabrics, but it was her style. She didn't look at me. Her gaze moved methodically from the panel to her notes, never once crossing mine. The precision in her eyes was mechanical. It was the kind you'd see in a supervisor inspecting a machine she'd built herself, already aware which part was about to fail. She didn't need to think about me because she was the only one in the room that already knew me.

Jolin and I had been inseparable once. We'd entered the department the same year at MIT as young, ambitious scholars, both dreaming for recognition. Our advisor used to call us "the twins," what he described as two halves of a single sharp mind, wired to the same logic, the same instinct. Back then, it felt less like a friendship and more like a mirror, that would eventually learned how to look away.

But the truth was, we'd never really been friends. We were rivals disguised as friends. Or maybe that was only how it felt, beneath the civility and shared applause. She was brilliant, disciplined, and always seemed to have a second plan—just like the presentation she'd given before mine. I was restless, forever testing the edges of the field. We admired and despised each other in equal measure, but also bound by the same hunger that taught us to coexist in peace.

"This is a conference on the science of linguistics, Mr. Lumen," Caroline said at last, folding her hands like she held the final say, because she did. "We're here for rigorous research, not art projects. Do you understand what presenting this does to the credibility of your work, and to the reputation of the international research community?"

That last sentence gutted me.

To be honest, the paper had taken three sleepless years of field trips, drafts, revisions, and rejections, clawed back through endless rounds of peer review before it was finally accepted into the conference, though only as a 'weak accept.'

What started as a salvage project on a dying Pacific tongue in the Solomon Islands had slowly unraveled into nothing. The recordings were fragmented. The transcriptions, incomplete and inconsistent. Eventually, the department's funding ran dry. I took on extra teaching loads, even spent what remained of my scholarship, just to keep the project breathing a little longer.

And then came the talk of fast-tracking my academic profile. Invitations to appear as a co-author on papers I hadn't written. Requests to review manuscripts I barely skimmed. Offers to join editorial boards alongside names that looked good in print to offer a quiet assurance that I still belonged. It was all meant to keep me circulating in the system to make me look visible, credible, alive in the academic bloodstream.

They had faith in me. And hence, I couldn't afford to falter. Not for my department's sake, not for my own. But because once you're cast out of academia, you can't climb your way back in. You fade, citation by citation, until you're nothing but a forgotten reference.

I told myself I was modeling possibilities. I wasn't lying. I wasn't fabricating nonsense. The language might have been invented—that I admitted—but it was born from observation, intuition, and proven methodology from science. The data, the patterns, the structure were sound enough to withstand my advisor's scrutiny, even if their origin wasn't.

The last thing I wanted was for all that work to go down the toilet. Surely, there had to be a way to justify it to make it worthy since it was already accepted and published in a conference like this.

"I understand," I said, quickly. "But the cognitive framework—"

The moderator lifted a hand as if drawing a line under the moment and sat down. "Thank you, Mr. Lumen."

I stepped away from the podium, the projector light still fading on the wall behind me, my palms slick with sweat.

As I walked past the third row, Jolin's voice caught me like electricity brushing past. "You should've told me," she whispered, her eyes fixed on the stage the whole time.

"I didn't think I had to," I muttered under my breath, as I returned back to my seat, grabbing a bottle of water from the refreshment table on the way.

Jolin snorted. Not in a cruel way, but the kind of response that hides its sympathy because that's more painful to show.

△△△

I spent the rest of the afternoon drifting through the floors of 333 George Street like a ghost. I leafed through the conference program, scanning the talks and presentations, wondering whether my paper would still be published. I tried to push away the thought that the entire conference might be retracted because of me, even though it seemed the most likely and reasonable outcome.

Between sessions when attendees were forming social groups, I sat alone at the outside balcony back on level 13, and answered student emails and graded assignments. Half the messages in my inbox were protests from students claiming I'd miscalculated their marks, cited something wrong, or corrupted their files entirely. With every reply, the veil of student-teacher authority and professionalism thinned, one keystroke at a time. It was a quiet reminder that in this system, even control was temporary like another file waiting to be deleted.

I hadn't eaten any of the provided meals when lunch or afternoon tea was served. Everything on the tables contained either gluten, yeast, nuts, dairy, eggs, or excessive sodium. They were things my body – or more specifically, my skin – refused to tolerate.

I hadn't eaten anything since the ten-thousand-mile flight from Boston to Sydney, except for a small salad labeled *entrée* at a nearby restaurant. The few scraps of lettuce, cucumbers and avocado were the only thing safe enough to eat. Not to mention, cheap enough to justify.

While everyone else lingered over sandwiches, pastries, and coffee, I stayed anchored in my seat. My eyes were fixed on my laptop, pretending to look occupied with something academic, when really, I was just trying to keep my pulse from betraying me.

A couple of bottles of water were all I'd managed, and only because the catering staff had asked if I wanted anything. It wasn't just the allergies—but the act of eating itself that felt dishonest. Like rewarding myself before I even knew whether I'd been caught.

I sat through two more panels. One on phonetic shifts in endangered languages. The other on syntactic variation in emerging language varieties.

My mind was just not there and everything sounded flat and lifeless.

The thought unspooled into a quiet prophecy of ruin. I could already see the headlines with MIT's logo beside the banner: *PhD Fraud Scandal.* Google would cough up the evidence in endless scrolls of blog posts, forum threads, screenshots of my emails, and of course, the paper itself slashed with red ink printed 'RETRACTED'. Grants would vanish. Collaborators would recuse themselves. Committees that once nodded at my talks would meet in sealed rooms with civil faces and pitchforks in their hands.

My scholarship would be revoked. My advisor would sign the form to turn me from student to cautionary tale. Employers would type my name into a search bar and stop at the first result. Recruiters would delete my CV mid-scroll. Banks would file me under 'too risky', and landlords would stop returning calls. The visas and fellowships I'd planned my future around would be automatically rejected. Friends would fade, not with malice, but because it was easier to do so.

I wouldn't just fail my PhD. I'd be erased from it. Every citation I'd ever earned would be withdrawn, every mention redacted. At the end, all that will remain was a blank space where a career used to be.

It would take only one of these people to make the first move before the domino effect took everything down. Suddenly, my career felt like glass. One accusation, and it would be beyond repair.

I was already in my thirties, still drifting from one uncertain position to the next. No tenure. No anchor. Nothing to fall back on if this went under. I was always a step behind, as if time itself had moved on without me.

By the time I noticed my laptop was dying, the room had already emptied. The sunlight had shifted, casting long, slanted shadows like prison bars across the conference tables like bruised marks. It felt as if even the room itself ached from my presence. Through the windows, I could see office workers on the floors above, drifting into elevators.

But in my head, only a couple of seconds had passed since being exposed in front of more than 50 people. If I were a game character, this would be the moment the screen hung on a single image, the music fading out, a single line of dialogue looping until I finally chose what to do next. So what would I do? That was something I still hadn't worked out.

As the first day of the conference wound down, the staff moved quietly through the room, packing up around me. I stayed in my seat, adrift in the question, until the sound of the cleaner switching on the vacuum cleaner reminded me I should be heading back to the ground floor.

In the lobby, near the exit, a long table waited beneath the dim lights. It was stacked with free logo-stamped notebooks, tote bags, boxes of sponsor snacks, and the published conference proceeding this one. I was just about to slip through the automatic doors by myself when one of the staff members looked up from the table and called my name.

I turned around.

The catering staff smiled nervously. "You're Jarvis, right? Someone left this for you."

It was a small white box, about the size of my hand, small enough to slip into a pocket. A dark red ribbon was tied around it, pulled tight enough to leave creases like the faint lines of the inside of a rose.

"Who was it?" I asked, cocking my head.

"She didn't say," the staff member replied awkwardly, as she began packing the leftover merchandise gifts from the table. "But I think her name was Jolin."

I managed a brief, polite upturn of my mouth.

Of course.

Outside, the air carried the faint scent of an Italian restaurant across the road, drifting through the fading heat still trapped in the concrete. I found a bench along George Street and sat down, watching tourists and locals bounce their shopping bags and small talk through the cooling air.

The light rail rattled along the tracks with its bells chiming. Across the street, the glass facade of the post office reflected the fading orange light of late afternoon, while in the distance, the spires of the Queen's Victoria Building caught the sun's last rays.

I untied the ribbon of the small box on my lap.

Inside was a neatly sealed pack of vegan, sugar-free chocolate from Dubai, sweetened only with freeze-dried apple slices. The wrapper was a pale metallic gold, the text printed in both English and Arabic, the surface catching the light like tarnished silver.

Beneath the chocolate was a folded note written in Jolin's elegant, slanted hand.

I know you didn't eat much due to your allergies. I remember your skin breaks out. Here's something safer.

– Jolin

P.S. I think you did a great job!

For a moment, I didn't know whether to laugh or cry.

CHAPTER 2
PARANOIA

The next morning, I woke before dawn. Maybe it was jet lag, though I doubted it. I hadn't slept properly since arriving, not even during the day, so I should have been craving sleep no matter the hour. Still, I forced myself to return to the conference, even though every part of me wanted to disappear and let the world move on without me.

Maybe the humiliation would sink under the weight of morning coffee, new name tags, and the polite academic chatter pretending everything was fine. Maybe Professor Caroline Stone would come up to me, say she'd read my paper, and admit that the language I'd fabricated had real merit. That it grew out of rigorous research. That the journal was sound after all. That I might have stumbled into an entirely new subfield of research. Maybe she would take me aside, point me in a better direction, and all of this would become nothing more than a difficult origin story I could someday tell students under my supervision.

Inside, the lobby caught the morning light and fractured it into sharp reflections. The atmosphere vibrated with the restless murmur of voices, the snap of elastic bands from posters as presenters set up their displays, and the dry rustle of freshly printed programs being handed out by the conference staff.

I moved through the familiar corridor, past the registration desks cluttered with fresh name tags, past the polished conference tables littered with microphones and half-empty cups, past rows of academics bent over notes and glowing laptop screens, their badges swinging as they hurried between sessions.

I waved, but nobody looked at me.

Nobody noticed me.

Nobody spoke to me—except for the same staff member from yesterday, who came by again to ask if I wanted more water, and gave me the extra option of hot or cold.

I sat near the back of level 13, trying to make myself a small and invisible just-another-face in the crowd. I avoided everyone's eyes, afraid of what I might see in them, and waited for someone else to speak first. The presentations went on as if I'd never been there yesterday at all.

My only sense of the room came from the reflections. I couldn't avoid the weary eyes glancing off laptop screens. There were also the faint faces bending in glass panels, and the ones rippling on the surfaces of reusable tumblers. They all seemed to look straight at me.

I studied the staring faces through distortions where no one could look back and wink. The reflections shimmered in fragments, as if reality itself were trembling. Their eyes were wide, too glassy, impossibly still. Unblinking in a way that felt deliberate, almost sentient. Lips were drained of color, stretched into crooked smiles that couldn't possibly hold teeth.

Some mouths in the reflections hung slightly open, revealing wet tongues a few shades darker than they should have been. Their expressions were frozen in impossible combinations, like half-smiling, half-frowning tentacles with thousands of small suctions my mind shouldn't have been able to see.

I shivered, my stomach tightening.

I blinked once, hard, and the hallucination snapped back.

The eyes were back to the usual shades of brown, blue and green, blinking in ordinary humanity as expected. The lips had color once more, matching the faces they belonged to. Smiles and frowns now moved in perfect sync with their real expressions. The pause was gone. The distortions, the impossible combinations of teeth and lips like appendages all vanished, replaced by something far more ordinary.

When I looked at the actual people, they weren't staring. They were absorbed, leaning forward in their chairs, scribbling notes, asking questions about grammar rules, sentence structure, word meanings, and pronunciation patterns.

By the afternoon, I realized I couldn't do it.

I was no longer part of the conference. I couldn't even consider myself a spectator.

I didn't think I could go back the next day either. The shame had lodged itself deep, and the hostile silence from everyone around me only made it worse.

No calls. No messages. Nobody cared. I was on my own.

The rest of the conference passed without me. I slipped out when morning tea began, carrying only my water bottle, refilled from the dispenser. I told myself everything was fine, and for a moment, even believed it.

I wandered the streets of Sydney, not caring where I went.

I drifted past the sandstone buildings across the road near Martin Place, where office workers grabbed flat whites from the local coffee shop and checked their Opal cards before hopping on the trains below.

I began to wonder what I would do with my career now. Should I quit my PhD and at least call it as a decision, not a defeat? My savings were dwindling after I'd used my own money to fund research trips—including this conference. All I had left were a few stock options and whatever remained in my account. Each month the numbers had been slipping lower steadily and unforgivingly, like a quiet slope I couldn't stop sliding down. Lately, I'd grown afraid to even check the balance.

Everywhere I looked, reflections continued to follow me, caught in the glass of office towers, in the mirrored faces of shop windows. I told myself I was fine. That people survived worse. Maybe this was just another low point, another phase before things evened out, though deep down I knew I was lying.

I moved through Chinatown, weaving between tourists and the steam rising from restaurant windows. My reflection flickered across shopfront glass and the bronze flanks of the guardian lion statues, then followed me down toward the harbor, where the scent of salt hung in the air and faces stared back from under bicycle helmets and the oily sheen of the water.

The faces that looked back weren't anyone I knew. They were strangers with too-steady eyes and smiles that stopped halfway. Their silent attention pressed against me until every glance felt like a quiet accusation.

I told myself it was exhaustion.

Paranoia.

But there was something about all of them. Something I couldn't name.

It was something like the story my mother used to tell me about Robin Hood. Wolves in the forest would wear the king's armor, blending in until you didn't see the wolves until it was too late. Maybe that was what these reflections were. They were wolves, blending in, watching, waiting.

Only now, I felt like I was the prey, and the forest was alive with eyes, judging, waiting, tracking every step I took.

When I turned from the reflections to the real people, they weren't staring. They were taking selfies, licking ice cream, feeding seagulls. Oblivious.

By late afternoon, I found shade under an overpass near Barangaroo and slumped on the concrete with the view of the Sydney Harbor Bridge stretching toward the city skyline. My bottle of water had gone warm. The city moved around me, but I felt like a melted snowflake.

But for what? And why did it feel like I couldn't escape these reflections?

I laughed quietly to myself.

"You're just tired," I whispered.

That night in my hotel on George Street, I slept maybe maximum three hours. Probably less. I sat by the window, shoulder against the sill, staring at my reflection against the city beyond the Queen Victoria's Building. The nearby bars and restaurants below my hotel were nearly empty. If I was gone, no one would notice.

For a long time, I just watched, convincing myself I was tired, drained, and too small to matter in the rush of the biggest city in Australia. It was me. And it wasn't. Shadowed eyes, a tight mouth, shoulders slumped with exhaustion. A faint rash lingered across my face, subtle but restless, caught somewhere between healing and spreading.

I had treated my research like a game of strategy, predicting how academics would read it, how they would respond, how one misstep could reveal everything. Every nuance, every vowel shift, every morphological quirk had been calculated like a mental chessboard played out in my head. I knew one wrong move and the truth would be exposed.

And yet, despite all that effort, it had been exposed anyway.

For a moment, I swear the reflection stared back. The look wasn't accusatory. It wasn't cruel. It was knowing. It was as if it understood something I could never prove true, even after a hundred hypotheses and tests. Something about the wolves. Something about the things that follow you after you've humiliated yourself.

But at least the reflection didn't judge me. It mirrored the exhaustion, the desperation of undoing a mistake, the careful energy I'd spent constructing a lie so intricate I had almost convinced myself it could survive scrutiny.

It was a forbidding recognition of the game-theory chess I'd played against peers and reason itself. It was the cost of the sleepless nights, of the trans-Pacific flight, of grading MIT students' work overtime on top of everything else.

I leaned closer.

The lights in the street shimmered across the glass. My reflection's lips moved slightly. A smirk formed that I didn't make. I blinked, and it was gone.

I sucked in a breath and felt like wax too close to the flame.

In a few days, I'd have to face the university, my advisor, maybe the dean. But tonight, I let the exhaustion settle into my bones, let the city sound engulf around me until I was truly invisible.

But somewhere between pride and ruin, there was a small, quiet space where I could still breathe. And in that space, I whispered a word from my invented language—that even now, still had no name—that I should have let go.

The language didn't exist anywhere but in my mind.

And that, I decided, was enough for now.

CHAPTER 3
INITIATE

By day three, the conference was over. I hadn't met anyone. No one had reached out to ask about my absence. No one had asked for my email, what software I used to transcribe my recordings, or what made me so interested in linguistics. It was as if I'd already begun to fade from the frame.

I had wanted to linger an extra day, maybe explore the outer suburbs of Sydney a little with a tour group and make some new friends that way. But the thought of navigating a city where the streets curved the wrong way and the people spoke in accents I couldn't quite catch was exhausting.

Then there were the food allergies that acted like a quiet barrier that kept me from walking into a restaurant with the others, sitting down, talking, and eating before moving on with the next itinerary. Even something as simple as sharing a meal felt like another reminder that I was better off alone.

I cut the trip short. I used a public phone to rebook my flight back to Boston, despite the additional airline fees. It still seemed cheaper than staying longer. At least that's what I told myself as I listened to the hollow dial tone between calls.

I just wanted to leave, and do anything to make me feel anchored again.

I stepped off the train and into Sydney International Airport with a single piece of luggage and a packet of baby carrots I'd bought on sale at a corner grocer. But who was I fooling? If I'd had the luxury of eating whatever I wanted, without consequence, I wouldn't feel this hollow, even as I was heading back home.

My skin itched, my limbs ached.

The mental weight of sleepless nights, the backlog of ungraded work clogging MIT's learning system, and the humiliation of the conference pressed down on me like wet cement setting in the cold. Around me, the airport pounded with the screech of trolleys and the flicker of departure screens. The air reeking of duty-free perfume and disinfected surfaces didn't help either.

I needed a quiet corner, somewhere to sit without eyes on me. A business lounge looked like the perfect temporary refuge. My boarding pass was for the cheapest economy seat I could find with no extras. But for a moment I caught myself wondering if a space alone might be worth paying for if the price was reasonable.

Despite the maze of signs and the blur of rushing staff, I eventually found the lounge after finishing my packet of baby carrots, my legs aching from the walk. It sat tucked away on a quiet mezzanine beneath the chaos of Terminal 1, beside an abandoned shoe-polishing kiosk and a dark, unattended currency exchange desk.

The lounge was not tied to any airline. No flashing signs, no emblem, and no cheerful attendant waving in weary travelers. Even the windows were missing, leaving no way to tell whether it was day or night outside, or if it was rain or sunshine. It felt strangely neutral like a hidden corner of calm amid the airport's constant motion.

I entered the reception area and handed my boarding pass to the man behind the desk.

"Welcome, I'm Brendan," the staff member said, taking my boarding pass as he casually chewed gum. His smile looked forced and never reached his eyes.

His uniform was purposely styled the way a teenager might wear it with one side of his shirt untucked. His eyes widened slightly as he scanned my information, then tightened back into neutrality.

"Jarvis," he said softly, just enough that I blinked. "That's you?"

He studied the screen as his fingers hovered over the keyboard.

Then he smiled faintly and pressed a button I couldn't see, as if erasing something private.

"Follow me." He stepped away from the desk, toward the glass doors leading into the lounge.

I swallowed and looked through the door as it opened.

Inside, the lounge had clusters of soft leather chairs arranged like Tetris cubes. Warm golden light reflected off the glass partitions, and the marble floor gleamed underfoot.

I thought back to my economy boarding pass. I was certain it was a budget fare with no extra legroom, no checked luggage, no meals—and certainly no business lounge privileges. And yet, here I was, being welcomed in. No one asked for my credit card. No one mentioned prices or options. How could that be? Had I somehow forgotten it was my birthday and accidentally activated some special promo? Something must have gone wrong, or maybe it was an omen that returning home was the right choice after all.

But before I moved, Brendan looked back at me. "Where were you born, by the way?" he asked.

"Boston," I answered cautiously.

"And the time?" he asked, standing firmly in the opened door, his eyes rising briefly, scanning me as if measuring something I couldn't see.

"I believe 1 a.m." I frowned. "Why?"

"Just checking." He paused, studying me intently. "Sun, moon, and rising—Taurus, Pisces, Capricorn. Am I correct?"

"Astrology?" I froze, utterly confused. "All I know is that I'm a Taurus."

Brendan didn't answer. He only gave a weak, almost knowing smile, as if my confusion was exactly what he expected.

"Don't worry," he replied with a laugh, like he had expected that.

We walked past the other guests into the quieter interior of the lounge.

He led me toward the seating area filled with low tables and a spread of all-you-can-eat pastries and fruits. There was coffee brewing in silver carafes, complete with cinnamon, cocoa, and nutmeg toppings. Bowls of mints rested on every counter, and a neat selection of glossy periodicals fanned out beside the armchairs.

He glanced at the other passengers already settled in the lounge. Some of them were scrolling through tablets, sipping coffee or leafing through magazines. But he ignored them entirely.

A man who had just arrived near the reception desk was shouting about something, but Brendan didn't even look at him once.

Instead, he directed me to a table. It could have been any table. But somehow the one he chose for me felt intentional. It was like it had been set aside just for me. The surface was a deep walnut gloss, so smooth without a wrinkle or scratch it made me think it had only just been brought in. It smelled faintly of lemon and berry. Maybe it was recently cleaned. Maybe it was quieter. I didn't know why anyone would think I deserved that.

I sat down and placed my bag on the small table.

Brendan leaned slightly against the edge of the table, fidgeting under his sleeves, still watching me with that precise, deliberate attention I couldn't get over.

"You look worn out," he said softly, his eyes lingering over me like a stubborn haze. "Long day? Or… did something go wrong? Maybe a shock with how things work here in Australia compared to back in the States?"

"You could say that," I admitted, sinking into the chair.

"You're a linguist, right?" his voice was casual, but his eyes held an intensity that made me uneasy.

"Yeah… how did you—"

"The badge," he said, pointing toward my conference name tag still glued to my shirt. "It gave me a hint. Several people from the conference have passed through here the last few days, but something about you stood out."

I sank deeper into the chair, feeling exhaustion press even harder as the reminder of the humiliation rushed back.

Brendan didn't flinch. He didn't blink fast. His attention never wavered.

"I'll leave you to it," he said, his tone warm as he walked back to the reception desk, passing by a self-service drink station that had the list of departing flights above it. "Rewind a little. Grab a drink, have a shower, do whatever you need. I won't judge. It's going to be a long flight, and you look like you haven't slept in days."

For the first time since the conference, I felt seen. I was not mocked, nor ignored. I was observed with deliberate focus and dignitary.

A barista asked if I wanted a cup of coffee. I said water would be fine.

I thought about moving to one of the reclining chairs. Maybe slip into the dim cinema room where the news played on repeat. But I stayed where I was, upright at the table with my half-empty cup, watching Brendan adjust his cuffs and smooth his sleeves. His movements were casual, but I could tell he was on high alert as he listened to the man fuming by the reception desk. I couldn't explain why, but I knew the man wasn't just waiting to be served, he was looking for someone.

CHAPTER 4
SEDATION

Brendan appeared suddenly next to my table again. He didn't call my name. He didn't make a sound. He just leaned lightly against the table like before, watching me with the same measured patience that made me feel this was beyond what he was trained to do.

His sleeves were rolled down. His hands were neatly folded around a bottle of expensive-looking wine that looked unopened. The way he stood attentively spoke of years in hospitality experience. Maybe not quite ten years yet, but close enough to make him a professional. Probably a few years less than I'd spent in academia.

"I've got a vacant private room with a private bathroom and shower if that's something you're interested in," he said, his voice low, without urgency, but carrying a subtle insistence that made me stiffen. "It's usually an extra $60 more."

Even with the stronger exchange rate, sixty dollars felt like a part of me I'd never see again. Every bill I handed over seemed to vanish into a void, and I couldn't shake the thought that one day soon, there'd be nothing left. My research career was already slipping through my hands no matter how tightly I tried to hold it.

"I don't think I can afford it," I admitted.

"No, I mean its free of charge," Brendan replied, and relaxed his shoulders. "For you only."

"Free?" I repeated, unsure if I heard right.

"Look at it as a treat from me," Brendan said.

There was a controlled grace in the way Brendan moved as he led me toward the rows of private suites behind the self-service drink station. Whether it was an act or genuine, I was still unsure. Every gesture felt rehearsed. It was the kind of attentiveness that made me feel seen in a way that bordered on intrusive. It was the sort of treatment reserved for someone special. For a moment, I felt like a guest of honor. Maybe I was. And maybe that was the catch.

As he unlocked the door to my private room, he gestured toward the bottle in his hand. "Care for a drink? It's a 2016 Penfolds Grange."

Though I wasn't a drinker, the name itself was enough to land in my head. It was one of the most expensive wines from Australia. It was the kind you didn't just pour and gulp down, but unveiled over a special dinner.

"I would love to but I can't," I said finally, wishing I wasn't born with my allergies. "My skin—"

He nodded, unsurprised, like he'd expected it.

"What about tea?" he asked.

I shook my head again.

He studied me silently for a long moment, as though weighing something in his mind. "Do you want some lemon and cucumber slices in water then?"

"Just filtered water will be fine."

△△△

The private shower was a small miracle, even though I had to angle my elbows several times to avoid the cold tile to access the soap dispensers. Still, the water ran hot and had good pressure. The steamy warmth cascaded over my skin, washing away airport grime, and the lingering anxiety of the conference. I could feel the tension in my shoulders uncoiling, the tightness in my chest reviving.

For a moment, I thought I might actually feel human again. But even as the heat seared the grime from my skin, the crawling, writhing sensation of a million soft-bodied things squirming beneath the surface of my pores retained.

My arms, my neck, my back seemed to creep no matter how much I scrubbed.

I had barely stepped out of the shower when a knock echoed through the room. The warmth still clung to my skin as I reached for a towel. Before I could answer, Brendan stepped inside again, unannounced.

In his hand was a cup of water. He stirred it, his eyes never leaving mine. Inside the cup, the ripples spread in tight, perfect circles, trembling against the edges as if trying to escape. I realized I hadn't held eye contact with anyone in days, much less not with someone like him.

"It's just filtered water, as you requested," he said in the same soothing tone as he placed the glass on the table beside the bed. He stood very close, so close I could feel the heat of his body, the faint sweetness of his breath, the sharp trace of hairspray lingering in the air between us. "If there's anything else you need, please do not hesitate to let me know, Taurus boy."

I lifted the glass and drank. The water was warm at the top but cold at the bottom. It had no ice. It carried no sour tang, no earthy grit, no chalky aftertaste. It was the flat, polished neutrality of filtered water, the way Brendan said it was.

At first, the room seemed perfectly ordinary. The pale walls, the neatly made bed, and the faint scent of vanilla and berry felt oddly comforting. Even the soft breeze of the air conditioner and the gentle mist from the humidifier drifted through the air like a lullaby.

But then I noticed them. I mean, I saw those tiny, pinprick-like eyes embedded in the texture of the walls, catching the dim light. At first, I thought it was just dust or static glinting on the surface. But then all the eyeballs moved at once, as though they were deeply intelligent and cunning.

The longer I stared, the more of them I saw. I swear there were a million of the little eyes, blinking in uneven rhythms beneath the paint, as if the walls themselves were breathing. Somewhere beyond the plaster came a faint rustle that was too soft to be footsteps, but too alive to be the wind.

I blinked, and they vanished.

I blinked again, and they were back, scattered across the walls.

The bed beneath me suddenly felt unstable, though I knew it hasn't moved.

A low, pulsing hum thrummed through the air.

My limbs felt like clay. My knees buckled, and my stomach twisted violently. I tried to cry out, to grab the bed, to speak. But nothing came out. The eyes seemed to follow every twitch my body made, like it was purposely, judging me.

I blinked again to rid myself of the hallucination. Or at least tried to.

Colors stretched and warped in high saturation, bending and shifting in impossible ways. The bed became liquid beneath me. The walls seemed to stretch in different proportions like jelly and sway, and Brendan's figure multiplied. His face fractured into overlapping images, one tired and pale, one impossibly alert, one with eyes sharp and focused.

I tried to look away from Brendan, but my gaze was locked and drawn to him.

And then the world went black.

CHAPTER 5
OTHERWISE

When I woke up, the first thing I did was rub my arms and hands. I braced for that raw, splitting pain that usually greeted me before I was even fully awake. It was the kind that told me something had triggered my skin again. Maybe it was food contaminated with gluten, a crumb left beside the toaster, or even fine dust in the air settling on a patch of skin too sensitive to defend itself. I expected the cracks, the dried blood, the faint tackiness of pus that never seemed to heal.

But this time, nothing.

The rashes that had tormented me for days were gone.

My skin was smooth and unblemished.

My heartbeat quickened.

Impossible—yet there it was, undeniable under my fingertips.

I sat up slowly, still dizzy. The berry scent that lingered in the air still felt comforting, but it was strangely edged with something sterile.

I collected my belongings, made sure to throw my empty cup in the trash, and headed toward the main entrance where I'd first come in.

Brendan was sitting at the reception desk, the glass door already open. His long sleeves were neatly covering his forearms. His hands were folded calmly. His gaze was fixed on me as though he had been waiting, timing my awakening down to the second.

"You're awake," Brendan said with a giant smile that stretched literally from ear to ear so that it looked like a mask.

"Thanks for the room and upgrade," I said to him, still running my hands over my impossibly clear skin on the way out.

Brendan tilted his head slightly. "I didn't offer you the room for free," he said, looking mildly confused. "You paid for everything with your leftover Australian dollars."

"I did?" I halted, unable to find the narrative to my memory that I did that. "But… I swear… you led me here to let me rest because you saw my skin wasn't looking so good."

"No?" Brendan looked even more confused, cocking his head as though it was his turn to question what really happened. "Your skin was already perfect when you arrived."

I opened my mouth to argue, but no sound came out.

Had my exhaustion warped my memory?

Had I really been as raw and desperate as I thought?

Brendan chuckled lightly and began typing something into the keyboard behind the reception desk, which I sensed was to cover a brief moment of awkwardness.

"Even I have sensitive skin sometimes," he added, lifting a sleeve to show a faint red rash in the fold of his arm. "Bodies don't always behave the way we expect, but we were programmed to heal."

I blinked, taking one step back into the terminal of the airport.

"By the way," he continued casually, "you seemed to be talking to yourself when you first came in. Are you feeling okay now?"

Talking to myself? I didn't remember that.

"Don't worry," he said, his voice smooth, practiced. "It happens to people in transit, under stress. You likely don't remember."

A wave of guilt passed through me, stemming from exhaustion, humiliation, and stress. Had I really muttered words I couldn't recall?

Maybe I did. Maybe I didn't.

"And one more thing." Brendan moved to a small table beside the lounge entrance and picked up a bottle of iced tea. He held it out toward me. "Don't waste this," he said. "Bring it onboard. You may need it."

I frowned. "Need it? For what?"

He shrugged and raised his arms. "You told me to save it for you—our little agreement, remember?"

I blinked, confused. "What? When?"

"Earlier," he said simply, amused. "Before you went to sleep."

The words hung there between us. What Brendan said felt unreal and impossible, yet the words were delivered with such certainty that I couldn't find fault with them.

My throat felt dry. I hesitated, then reached out and took the bottle anyway, its chill seeping into my palm. Maybe I'd agreed to give it to a friend, or a colleague, as some kind of souvenir. It was probably something I couldn't quite remember promising, like a slip of the tongue made while my mind was busy calculating how long I could sleep without missing my flight.

"For balance," he added, as though that explained everything, and pressed a button for the glass door to slide open into the terminal.

"Oh," I said.

"And if I ever see you again," he added lightly, "turn off the shower water before you sleep. You are definitely your sun, moon, and rising—Taurus, Pisces, Capricorn. All correct."

CHAPTER 6
MAYHEM

By the time I left the business lounge, I realized I had actually overslept. My chest sank. Somewhere between dozing and confusion, I had missed the announcements. The gate had closed, and the first leg of my flight—the one to Los Angeles before the layover to Boston—had long departed without me.

As I stared at the large departure board displaying all the flight schedules, I wondered how I could had slept so deeply. How could I have missed the boarding call? It couldn't be more than an hour, I convinced myself. It couldn't have been long.

If it had been a full day, I would have been asked to leave the lounge, forced out for overstaying. That hadn't happened. And Brendan had seen my boarding pass, so he was equally aware of my departure time. Anger began to sprout in my chest. If I had the choice between burning the bridge and watching it burn, I'd still pick the match.

My stomach churned anyway at the thought of lost hours, wasted travel, and the mounting frustration of having to rearrange my travel itinerary again.

I approached the airline service desk trying not to let my panic show.

"I missed my flight," I said, making it sound like it wasn't my fault. "Is there another one soon?"

The clerk was an old, fat woman whose expression suggested she'd seen too many travelers and cared for none. She gave me a quick once-over before tapping at her keyboard.

"Mr. Lumen," she said. "Mr. Jarvis Lumen. We called your name over the announcements several times, but you didn't come. Where were you?"

Her eyes scanned me up and down, and I caught a flicker of concern in them. She let out a breath of relief.

"Never mind," she said, clicking her tongue and sighing. "Let me see… Yes, there's one leaving in about an hour. But it's an extra $500. We can get you on it, but only if you're willing to pay."

I let out a breath I hadn't realized I was holding.

I had to remind myself that I still had overdue bills. Rent, utilities, internet, all stacked up like quiet threats. Maybe I could cut back somewhere, swap out the pricier groceries for cheaper ones, like fewer cashews, less almond milk, and maybe skip the imported fruit and buy rice in bulk instead. Boston wasn't exactly forgiving. My health insurance premiums were coming up, the credit card balance was already bleeding interest, and the student loan reminders kept arriving like clockwork.

The taxes, the transit pass, the overpriced streaming subscriptions, the endless little charges that crawled out of nowhere all wanted something from me. Everyone did, as long as it has something to do with me paying. It felt like everyone was wired to drain me dry, one automated payment at a time.

"That's too much," I said, anxiety crashing over me in soundless waves.

"Then you'll need to wait two days for the next free one," she said, voice heavy with the fatigue of someone who'd repeated the same line too many times. Then she looked up at me. "Look, I can charge you $300. There's a promo for American Express holders. I know you're not one, but I can apply it to your account. Will that make it work?"

At least this wasn't a total disaster.

At least, not yet. As they say, death by a thousand cuts takes time.

Agreeing to the promo, I returned to the terminal seating area and sank into a chair at my new gate number. My fingers drummed against the armrest, my restless nerves refusing to settle.

Next to me, a man around my age in a dark jacket caught my attention. One leg was wrapped in a damp bandage. Something thick and yellow was seeping through the gauze. Pus, I realized with a grimace. It looked like the kind of infection I knew too well, when my rash refused to heal and was attacked by bacteria.

He was absorbed in a newspaper, fingers trembling slightly as he turned the page. There was something odd about the calm intensity beneath his fatigue.

He glanced up briefly, his eyes sharp with no obvious expression of being injured.

"According to my astrology sign," he said, making his tone obvious that he was reading from the newspaper without preamble, "I'm supposed to suffer a setback today."

I blinked. "Your astrology sign?"

"Yes," he said, gesturing vaguely toward his bandaged leg. "Taurus. Minor disaster, a test of patience and resilience."

He shifted slightly, wincing as he attempted to cross his legs.

"Guess what, I'm a Taurus too." I swallowed. "I guess some fraction of humans experience setbacks each day. But 1/12 of everyone? That seems arbitrary, don't you think?"

"Exactly." He chuckled, dryly. "And yet here I am, part of the fraction. Sometimes it's unavoidable.

Sometimes when bad luck gets you, you can't even buy yourself a cup of tea."

I reached into my bag and offered him the small bottle I carried, the iced tea I never wanted. "Here. Maybe it'll help."

He looked at it, eyes curious. "What is it?"

"Lemon tea, which I coincidentally was just given," I said. "I can't drink it myself, but it's something you might enjoy. I also can't have too much sugar in my diet."

He smiled faintly. "Is this a precautionary measure, or for comfort?"

"Both," I admitted. Noticing the easy warmth in the way the conversation was unfolding, I added almost on impulse, as if to fill the silence before it turned, "I'm a linguist. I study words, stories, the ways people communicate, how language shapes the way we think. That's my work."

The man placed one hand on his injured leg.

"Then you'll understand why setbacks fascinate and frustrate me," he said, raising an eyebrow. "Believe it or not, I also studied linguistics in my first semester at college, but my dream of being an athlete took over. Physical resilience is my game. Yet here I am, undone by something so inevitable and fragile."

He laughed softly as he accepted my bottle. It was a dry laugh that made me feel a bit of sympathy for him. I also felt the tension in my own chest loosen a little.

Silence fell between us, broken only by the distant hubbub of the terminal, faint boarding announcements, and the crisp crack of a bottle opening as he took a long sip of iced tea.

I didn't notice any immediate change, but as I walked away from the waiting area to find a place to refill my water bottle, I glanced back at the man. He looked calm and almost serene as he innocently inspected the label on the bottle. And this was despite the damp bandage and the subtle tremor in his leg. There was no reason for me to suspect anything was wrong.

I walked toward the small shop near the terminal's central concourse, feeling the relief of movement. The coffee shops and rows of snacks and magazines grounded me after the strange tension of watching him. For a few minutes, I convinced myself that maybe the missed flight, the encounter, and the lingering unease from Sydney would finally dissipate.

I didn't know, of course, that this would be the last time I'd see the athlete alive.

CHAPTER 7
REFUGEE

I kept my eye mask on the entire flight as soon as I found my seat. I didn't take it off once. I didn't eat. I didn't drink. I didn't use the restrooms. Not when the cabin lights flicked bright. Not even when a flight attendant brushed past and asked if I wanted anything.

I just shook my head.

I didn't want to look at anyone.

I didn't want anyone looking back.

I kept thinking about the athlete at the airport. The bandage around his leg, the way it caught the light. I never even caught his name, yet everything else about him stayed vivid in my mind. His quiet voice. His slow smile. The way he lifted the bottle, said nothing, and drank.

He could have been my best friend. Maybe we'd already met somewhere, several times even, and just never noticed. Then came the paramedics, the commotion, the way people turned and whispered as if something irreversible had happened. I couldn't make out their words, only the expressions on their faces, and I saw they carried a kind of pity I couldn't bring myself to meet.

What if it had been me? What if I'd done that?

The bottle had been from Brendan, the lounge attendant.

The same man who had offered me "just water."

My stomach knotted every time I thought about it. I hadn't meant to hurt anyone. I didn't even know if anything was wrong with the drink. But if there was —if something had been in it—then I had handed it over. My fingers, my voice, my casual kindness, had been the delivery mechanism.

So I wore the mask, hoping it would make me invisible. I hid behind it, like it could shield me from guilt or recognition.

I didn't sleep at all during the 15-hour flight. I took ten milligrams of melatonin, then a little more. When that proved futile, I reached for a couple of allergy tablets that had always been able to pull me under. But nothing could quiet the anxiety threading through my thoughts and flooding every chemical reaction in my body until even exhaustion felt unreachable.

During my layover in Los Angeles, I kept to the far corners of the terminal, eyes fixed on the departure board, making sure I didn't miss the next flight. If I did, it would mean spending even more money I didn't have to spare. The announcements blurred into a background murmur, and the frantic people rushing to and from their flights were just silhouettes moving between duty-free shops and phone charging stations.

I must have looked insane. I was hunched over with my eye mask still on, muttering under my breath. My body buzzed like I'd been overdosed on caffeine even though it was all natural. I didn't dare look at any of the surveillance cameras scattered across LAX because some part of me was convinced that if I did, they'd recognize me, or worse, remember me.

My mind kept looping back to the same reel like a rattling movie: the athlete's bandage around his leg, the way he drank from the bottle, and then his body bag.

I boarded the connecting flight with a severe piercing pain in my head. The plane hummed softly. It was white noise that only made the inside of my skull ring even louder. I wanted to pass out, to stop existing for a few hours.

But instead, I just sat there, wearing my eye mask, feeling the weight of unseen gazes pressing down on me.

Someone across the aisle popped open a bottle of champagne and clapped their hands. The sharp crack made me flinch before I could stop myself. It obviously wasn't a gun, or a taser, or the metallic snap of handcuffs, but my body reacted anyway, primed for arrest before reason could catch up.

I tried not to look, but the temptation was hard to resist. I peeled the side of my eye mask, just enough to see the golden liquid fizzing in the glass.

The glass reflected the cabin lights like a warped mirror. I saw faces in it, like the ones back in the conference. Suddenly they were watching me again, whether they thought I knew it or not.

Their eyes moved with that quiet precision people have when they've seen something they wish they hadn't. It was a glance that lingers a beat too long like a half-swallowed signal. Or the subtle tightening at the mouth before hastily looking away. One of them might have known me from the conference, but I doubted it.

Still, someone always knows someone. Say the right name, and the whole web begins to unravel like a map. I could already hear their voices in some future interrogation: *He was strange. Barely moved. Didn't talk to anyone.* Their hands would freeze halfway through gestures, their voices dull, their eyes flick toward me and then away. It was the small things that betrayed humankind. They'd seen me. They'd remember me. And that would be enough.

I blinked hard, told myself it was exhaustion. Hallucinations.

It was like my mind was punishing me for the guilt I refused to confess. But when I blinked again, they were still there, glaring from the curves of the bottle, from the sheen of a metal tray, from the dark gloss of a touchscreen.

Every reflection in the cabin seemed to carry the same unspoken verdict: *You did this. You have cheated. You should leave.*

My pulse spiked. I tugged the blanket tighter around my shoulders. Someone brushed past me and I jerked. I just needed the flight to end. I needed the world to go still again, just long enough for me to breathe.

"We are about to land in Boston," the captain's voice broke through the cabin, announcing our descent.

The moment the wheels touched the ground, I unbuckled before the sign turned off. I didn't wait for the seatbelt chime. I didn't wait for permission. I didn't wait for anyone. Not the shuffle of bodies or the soft applause that sometimes follows survival. I was already halfway to the exit, hearing the hiss of the cabin door unlocking, the flight attendants' voices thanking us for flying.

When the door finally opened, I was the first out, half-running, half-stumbling down the aisle, still wrapped in the airline blanket like some lunatic refugee.

I didn't care what anyone thought. I didn't care if security stopped me for thinking I was under the influence. I needed to move, needed to get away from that pressurized metal coffin and the faces inside it.

The jet bridge tilted slightly under my feet. I almost tripped. My legs felt weightless and moved too quick, as if my body had been outrunning my thoughts for hours. Each step struck the floor with a resonating thud. It was strange to be on solid ground again while everything inside me was still moving and falling.

When I reached the terminal, the crowd hit me like tsunami.

Hundreds of faces, tired and pale, shimmered beneath the flat glow of the ceiling light that seemed to drain more than it gave. For a second, it felt like they were all silently watching me too, retelling what had happened, rewriting the story in their own heads in a different POV. Their glances seemed to echo between them, each one sharpening what I'd done, amplifying it, until even the way I stood felt like proof, I was a stereotypical madman in a movie.

I could almost see it again. Everything from their eyes shifting, lips mumbling, reflections of something I couldn't name staring from the polished floors where luggage wheels hissed and trolleys clattered.

I pulled the blanket closer. The fibers itched against my neck, but it made me feel protected.

No one stopped me.

No one called out my name or pointed at me.

I kept waiting for the shout, the heavy hand on my shoulder, and the accusation.

But nothing came.

It was just the crackle of distant announcements, the low grind of conveyor belts shifting luggage, and the ordinary rhythm of an airport in the late evening.

Still, I couldn't shake the thought that maybe I was being followed. That someone had seen me at the gate, remembered my face, and would piece it all together later.

The linguist. The man from the conference that falsified his research. The one with the poisoned drink.

I pushed through the exit doors into the cold Boston air. It hit me like a slap. For a moment, I thought I might cry. Not from grief or guilt, but from relief, from exhaustion, and the sheer absurdity of being home again.

Boston.

The city that had made me.

The city that was supposed to mean safety.

I crossed the curbside traffic with the blanket still wrapped tightly around me, its frayed end dragging and darkened by grime. I ignored that there could be drivers and passengers watching from behind their windshields, unsure if I was lost or contagious.

My heart wouldn't slow down. The reflections wouldn't leave me alone.

Every car window, every chrome surface seemed to twist and warp into faces with flared nostrils and hungry eyes. They were there and then gone again when I blinked, like the world was flickering between two versions of itself.

I told myself none of it was real. Everything would be fine when I reached Beacon Hill and settled back into my apartment after 24 hours of flying.

By the time I reached the taxi line, my lungs were raw, and my legs unsteady, moving on memory rather than will. I didn't feel pain, just that hollow exhaustion that comes after too much silence. And perhaps that why it felt so uncomfortable. The blanket was still safely around me, clinging like it knew what it meant to be left behind.

A driver leaned out of his window, eyes wide like he'd seen the impossible.

"Man, you okay?" he asked, half-laughing, half-alarmed. "You been running after me for like literally 100 blocks!"

I blinked. "What?"

"Yeah," the driver replied, his thumb tilted to the back of the car, as though to point towards the direction of Boston International Airport. "You chased me halfway across the airport lot. I thought you were going to collapse, but you just kept going. Then suddenly you were already at Beacon Hill before I even realized you weren't in the car."

My hands were shaking so badly I had to grab the door to steady myself. "I… ran… here?"

He nodded, looking at me like I was either a miracle or a maniac.

"Fastest thing I've ever seen, I swear," he said.

I didn't know what to say, but I was glad that I managed to save on the taxi bill.

My chest heaved, my heart was hammering.

The city lights of Boston blurred behind him as he drove away. I saw the familiar streets, cobblestone edges, gas lamps glowing soft orange.

Somehow, for the first time in my life, I had crossed all that distance on foot.

I approached my apartment building, the airline blanket still around my shoulders. The concierge pressed the entry button without a word, and I passed through the doors as if moving through a dream. Upstairs, my door had a drift of envelopes gathered at its base. I sifted through them: bills, bank statements, the usual junk promising rewards no one ever receives. Nothing from the university. Nothing from the conference. Nothing from the crime squad.

Everything inside my apartment felt the same. The same muted glow from the recessed ceiling lights still spilled across the wooden floors. The same wide screen TV hung like a dark mirror on the wall. The same couch, the same careful arrangement of pillows and folded throws, waited exactly as I had left them before I left for Australia. Even the air felt preserved.

As I looked out the window toward the quiet street and the curve of Boston Common below, I caught a faint glimpse of myself in the glass, superimposed against the city beyond.

And for a split second, my reflection didn't move the same way I did.

CHAPTER 8
RECONCILIATION

The next morning at breakfast, I managed only a single spoonful of silken tofu with rice. In the fruit bowl, an avocado had begun to soften, its cut surface darkening. Beside it, a banana browned quietly in the open air, the stem cracked but the peel otherwise untouched.

Giving up on eating, I stood in front of the mirror in the bathroom, rehearsing what I'd say to my PhD advisor. They were words that could decide everything. I'd been thinking about it all night and during my morning shower. Whether I'd stay in the program or sink under debt. Whether I'd walk out of MIT with a future, or with nothing but the wreckage of what I'd tried to build. If I was lucky, maybe he'd still keep me on his mailing list and be forwarded the occasional newsletter or conference announcement. Or maybe he'd just say he didn't know me at all.

The moment I finally felt confident enough to face the day, I realized my weekly meeting with my advisor at MIT was in ten minutes. I thought about catching the train, but I still wouldn't make it in time. A taxi was out of the question. My body was still wired from the flight, my legs had begun to tighten, and my lungs felt like sandpaper, but I chose to run anyway.

I sprinted down the narrow, uneven bricks of Charles Street, and past the State House's golden dome catching the cold morning light. I weaved through the last of Beacon Hill's side streets, then pushed onto Cambridge Street and barreled toward the Longfellow Bridge.

My legs pumped like never before as I raced across the bridge, leaving Beacon Hill behind, charging straight toward MIT. The Charles River sparkled beneath me as I ran, and I wondered if I would make it on time. I watched Cambridge's skyline slowly rose in the distant as I passed through professors and students heading to their morning classes.

By the time I reached the steps of MIT's Building 10, my hair was plastered to my forehead and my chest rose and fell with each strained breath. I had cut straight across the lawn, interrupting campus tours snapping photos in front of the famous dome. The weight of my bag pulled at my shoulder, reminding me how far I'd run.

I paused at the threshold of the Infinite Corridor, the famed artery that connects the university's primary buildings. A public thoroughfare by tradition, its walls were lined with metal cabinets and glass cases displaying the artifacts of student clubs, state-of-the-art innovations and experiments, and biographies of distinguished alumni.

I hurried down the corridor, hoping to make it to Vincent's office before the meeting began.

Vincent, my PhD advisor—and the only one my age who somehow acted older than he was, in that strange, unsettling way—had always been a calming presence. A few years ago, after completing my master's degree, I had no idea what to do next. I asked my graduate coordinator for advice, and she sent a mass email to a dozen potential advisors looking for PhD students to supervise.

I remembered it clearly because only Vincent replied. It wasn't one of those delayed responses that trickled in after weeks, but came within five minutes. The message was precise, professional, and already filled with possible research topics that were so polished it probably took him longer to write than the delay it took to send. It made me feel seen in a way no one ever had, except probably other than my own mother.

From that first email Vincent had sent me, I knew he was someone I could trust. He was sharp but understanding. He was the kind of person who seemed to already know who you were before you said a word. He'd studied up on where I went to high school, my GPA from my bachelor's, even the electives I'd chosen, long before our first meeting. He became a steady presence I relied on more than almost anyone.

I turned a corner of the Infinite Corridor and ran straight into someone with a bang.

"Oh—Jarvis!" Jolin exclaimed, stepping back quickly, adjusting her metallic sunglasses, shaped like slanted sun flares.

She was leaving Vincent's office, clearly in a rush, when I saw her. A familiar mix of surprise and awkwardness crossed her face. It was the same look she always had when caught off guard.

"I… didn't expect to see you here," she said, her voice lighter than usual, probably also due to jetlag. "Your plane just arrived last night?"

"It did," I muttered, trying to steady myself from the collision.

"I thought you decided to stay in Australia permanently." She laughed, taking off her futuristic sunglasses, like they belonged in a hip-hop music video rather than an academic hallway.

My thoughts were still spinning from the chaos around me. But then my mind flicked to the small, unexpected gift Jolin had given me back in Sydney just as I was about to leave the conference.

"Thanks… for that vegan chocolate from Dubai," I said, almost sheepishly, as if admitting it might break some unspoken rule.

Her eyes widened for just a fraction of a second as she swung the handle of her sunglasses in a full loop. A flicker of surprise or perhaps curiosity rippled briefly across her face before vanishing.

"How was it?" she asked immediately, her voice carrying a mix of warmth and something I couldn't quite place. "Did you like it? Did you eat it all in one go? Could you tell it was vegan? Would you like some more? It was expensive, but I thought you'd like it."

I nodded, refusing to admit that I hadn't touched it yet.

She offered a faint smile. She eyed me up and down excitedly. Then she darted down the hall as if pressed for time, leaving me with a strange mix of relief and lingering confusion.

For a moment, I almost forgot about the chocolate myself. I made a mental note to try it later today.

△△△

I drew a slow breath and stepped into Vincent's office. He was already seated at his desk with papers spread in that calculated disorder that passes for brilliance. On the monitor beside him he had my profile already open. I could see my own portrait, personal details, and every appointment and email thread displayed like a dossier he was proud to own.

The shelves lining his office walls were crowded with journals and conference proceedings I'd cited countless times during my time as an undergrad, their spines worn smooth from use. Between them sat a scattering of trinkets that looked as though they'd been cast in gold. A few designer briefcases rested neatly on the lower shelves, their European logos subtle but unmistakable.

Vincent took his eyes off the screen to greet me.

"Morning, Jarvis," he said, smiling a little too wide, his voice dipped in that practiced brightness people use when they're trying too hard to sound human. A sophisticated cologne of sandalwood and white musk lingered in the air. It was refined but deliberate, like everything about him. "We need to talk."

What now? My research—my carefully constructed data—was already proven falsified. Had the conference followed up? Had they sent a scathing email, a demand for correction, or worse, a public notice?

Before I could respond, the door swung open.

The dean, Simeon, barged in.

Simeon was older. Far older than Vincent and me, and he carried a presence that made the room feel smaller. His hair was mostly gray, streaked with black, sticking out at odd angles like antennae. His shirt was a plain white one, the kind from Target that didn't fit well. When he spoke, it was in a polished, posh accent where every syllable was measured in a way that made you straighten up without knowing why.

Simeon's eyes weren't just sharp. They also darted unpredictably, like they were constantly juggling ten things at once, and the way he looked at you could make even the smallest detail feel like a confession.

"What is this nonsense?" Simeon's voice boomed, sharp and furious, carrying decades of academic authority. "He was meant to be documenting an endangered language in the Solomon Islands, exactly as outlined in his thesis title and research questions. That was the condition of his scholarship, not wasting time on some… some… fantastical invention!"

My mind immediately jumped to the worst-case scenario he was about to spill next, like being expelled, or losing my scholarship. Or worst, being officially flagged for academic misconduct and being branded in the system in a way that could follow me for years.

All those thoughts of Sydney, the airport, the hallucinations, the death of the athlete all seemed to come crashing down at once again. And it made my head hurt.

Vincent leaned back slightly, almost amused, and folded his hands. His eyes flicked toward the Rolex on his wrist. It was a white-gold Daytona with a bezel studded in diamonds that caught the light like ice.

"Simeon, Jarvis isn't wasting our time," he said tolerantly, looking at the dean. "Jarvis has changed his approach. Our Jarvis is no longer simply trying to study dead languages. Jarvis is inventing new ones. But in order to do that properly, Jarvis has to study the old languages first. The methodology is rigorous, just… unconventional."

The dean's frown deepened, his hands gripping the edge of the table so tightly that his fingers turned white. He could have flipped the table over if he wanted.

"Unconventional?" Simeon roared, his face flushing crimson. He jabbed a finger in my direction, though his eyes stayed fixed on Vincent. "This is meant to be scientific, Vincent. Not some wish-washy project for Hollywood! Stories, fairytales have their place in Humanities, yes, but this is supposed to be academic rigor. You are his advisor, for God's sake! If he cannot produce measurable, verifiable results, then I will have no choice but to dismiss him from the program with a permanent academic misconduct."

"I'm sure we can work something out with Jarvis," Vincent replied.

"The board has decided he'll need to come up with a new research title," Simeon said sharply. "He has three weeks. Three weeks to prepare a new legitimate proposal for his candidacy presentation, or he's out and his scholarship will be cancelled. It must be ready. No time for a second revision. And if he fails," he added, his voice lowering, "he won't just lose his place here—he won't be employable in any academic department tied to this university. I've already had my assistant book the slot."

Three weeks.

The clock in my head started ticking madly.

But Vincent, unshaken as always, gave me a look that reminded me he was on my side.

Vincent leaned forward towards me, resting his elbows on the table.

"Jarvis, listen," he said, gesturing his hand for me to sit down on the chair in front of his desk. "You have potential. You've always had it. And yes, the approach is unconventional. Maybe it's even ahead of its time. But think about it. The signs are everywhere. Language is shifting, consciousness is evolving, and your work is right at the center of it. You just need to frame it cleanly and scientifically, but don't lose the pulse underneath. The rigor is already there. What's missing is recognition. What you're doing isn't a deviation, Jarvis, it's an awakening. It's still linguistics, but also living linguistics. The creativity isn't outside the research. It is the research."

The dean scoffed. "Creativity does not excuse fakeness, Vincent," he said, turning his eyes back to the door. "If it's not grounded in real research, it's meaningless. He has three weeks. That is all."

I nodded silently as I watched the dean mutter something under his breath, and angrily march out the room, leaving Vincent and me alone in the office, while my mind spun in a thousand directions.

Vincent leaned back, giving me that faint, reassuring smile only he could pull off. Perhaps it was his youth. Maybe the authority that came with a title far beyond what his age should allow. He was already an associate professor, and somehow, that only made his calm more disarming. Or perhaps it was because we had known each other for so long.

"Alright, enough doom and gloom," Vincent said. "There's another matter. Would you be interested in teaching a few more subjects? Lecturing, even? It could be a good opportunity to get further experience, and it will help clarify your own thinking about language."

I blinked.

Teaching. Lecturing. When my PhD—my main role as an academic in MIT—was beginning to crumble?

My heart skipped a beat, a mix of relief and dread.

The stress of teaching had already been a weight I carried everywhere, especially in Sydney, where I found myself stealing minutes between sessions to reply to student emails and argue over grades. The emails always came with the same polite outrage wrapped in academic language. I answered them on the plane, in bus stops, from quiet corners between conference talks, pretending I wasn't falling behind. By then, I'd already started wondering if the grind of teaching was worth the few extra few dollars it brought in.

Yet now Vincent was offering even more, piling on responsibilities I wasn't sure I could handle.

But Vincent's look didn't allow hesitation.

I swallowed hard.

"Do you really think this is the correct approach?" I said, voice steadying.

Vincent nodded, his expression almost conspiratorial, as if letting me in on a secret only we shared.

"That's settled, then," he replied, nodding, swaying in his chair to enter my name into a spreadsheet. "You'll get the schedule by tomorrow." He paused, eyes flicking up from the screen. "And Jarvis… remember, even the dean can't touch creativity if it's anchored in real work. I'm sure we'll have you back on your feet in three weeks. That's why I suggest you stop communicating with him altogether to prevent you from getting sidetracked."

"Ignore Simeon?" I asked, stunned by the advice. "So don't even read his emails?"

"That's correct," he said, with that same smile that always seemed capable of fixing anything. "Distance will make Simeon doubt his own reasoning. And when he reaches out, it'll be on your terms. In academia, you don't win by confrontation, but by disappearing long enough for them to recalibrate your absence."

I slumped into the chair, finally letting my breath out. I guess Vincent did have a point.

But Simeon's sudden demand to produce a new research title within three weeks, and Vincent's quiet insistence to push me deeper into the uncharted territory of teaching, were burdening me with more responsibilities than I had anticipated. Not to mention all the unsettling things in my chest.

And yet, somewhere beneath it all, a tiny spark of relief glimmered.

I wasn't expelled.

At least it didn't feel like I would be.

And I had a chance to prove that my strange, convoluted, sometimes terrifying ideas weren't worthless.

"Let's talk about the subjects you could teach," Vincent leaned back, steepling his fingers. "How about phonetics? Can you illustrate the vocal tract, tongue positions, and airflow clearly enough that students will truly understand?"

I shook my head quickly. "I don't think I want to teach another unit that requires drawing or even visualizing diagrams." My voice sounded smaller than I expected, even to me. "I simply am not a gifted artist."

Vincent leaned forward, eyes steady. "Remember, this is experience. It's credibility. It builds your track record. It's exactly what you need if you ever want a shot at a full-time academic position like me. Tenure, even."

Full-time academia? Job security? Academic freedom?

It sounded almost too good to be true.

"I'm trying to help you." A smile flickered across Vincent's face. "You have no idea how rare you are, Jarvis. I see what no one else does. I only push you because I care. You think I'd waste my time if you weren't worth it?"

I had to admit that Vincent's tone wasn't just persuasive. It was protective. He wasn't pushing for himself. He was pushing for me. Somehow, it felt like the ultimate goal that most, if not all, PhD students spend their careers chasing, especially in today's age when actually landing a tenure-track position after graduation is so rare.

"I'll do it," I said finally, my voice firmer. "I'll teach the subject."

Vincent's approving smile lit up on his face.

"I have faith in you," he reassured, the words landing slow and heavy. "You keep resisting, but you don't have to. The work is already happening. You just haven't opened your eyes yet."

"I know," I said, unsure what else I should say.

"Teaching will help you stay grounded, keep you tethered while your mind learns to expand," he repeated the same refrain. "Don't fight it, Jarvis. Stop resisting. The signs are all around you. You'll see them soon enough."

I leaned back in the chair, still feeling my heart hammering against my ribs. Why was I so tense? So wired? For the first time in days, it seemed like there was an unconditional glimmer of light at the end of a tunnel that had been meant to exist all these counterfeit years.

And yet, the nervous energy in my chest refused to ease, as if my body hadn't caught up with the hope my mind kept forcing on it. Somewhere inside, a smaller voice tried to speak, but I ignored it—I always did when it told me things I didn't want to hear.

CHAPTER 9
EPIPHANY

That night, after finishing what was left of my breakfast from this morning—the tofu, rice and avocado I'd left all day on the counter—the language crept into my mind in tonal and fragmented sequences I could barely recognize. It pulsed behind my eyes like a fever I couldn't tame.

The language that came flooding into my mind wasn't the one I'd studied or recorded during fieldwork in the Solomon Islands, or anywhere else in the Pacific. This one moved differently. It wasn't spoken so much as it *breathed*. It was alive, insistent, and wrong in an unearthly way that felt intimate. The sounds coiled with a rhythm I almost recognized, like a lullaby sung by my mother.

I spent the evening scribbling frantically in my notebook, while listening to old recordings of dying languages I'd recorded. They were interviews I'd conducted a year earlier that contained the fading voices of indigenous elders carrying traditional stories that now sounded like echoes from another life. It was sweet how they tried to remember every word, pausing, apologizing, starting again as though the language itself was fragile and needed care.

I tried to get my inspiration from these real languages, but I also didn't care that the language I was inventing sounded like nonsense. I kept inventing because I had to. Because Vincent believed in me the way a real advisor should, unlike Simeon.

As I traced the patterns and small rules of the new language, something shifted in my head. The chaotic pulse of tones and accents slowed, softened, and began to coalesce into a hypnotic rhythm. It was like the way great composers wrestle with raw notes until they emerge as symphonies.

The language had a structure that felt logical, yet flexible.

Its tones reminded me of Cantonese, where a single syllable could mean something completely different depending on whether the voice went up, down, or in between.

The thought took me back to the time I wandered the streets of Chinatown in San Francisco during a trip to a wedding at the Palace of Fine Arts. There, under lanterns swaying above narrow alleyways lined with red-and-gold shop signs, I soaked in the sounds of vendors and street performers, marveling at how a single word—like 'ma'—could change entirely depending on the pitch it was pronounced. The closest thing in English was the way a sentence's pitch rises for a question.

Those memories returned vividly now, and I realized I was drawing on them unconsciously.

But this new language forming in my mind didn't follow the rigid fixed-number tone system of Cantonese. Instead, it moved in dynamic contour chains, with tones gliding smoothly, rising abruptly, and falling unexpectedly, creating sequences that sounded musical. I realized this was a unique trait, and I resolved to preserve it.

Stress patterns worked differently too. In English, we naturally emphasize certain syllables in words, like in 'banana' or 'photograph.' But in this language, stress could shift depending on the speaker's intention, to let emphasis travel across a sentence, like conducting an orchestra. Thinking back to Russian, which I had studied for its rhythmic stress patterns, I could see the logic in its emphasis.

But in this new language, the stress moved fluidly, as though it held emotions of its own. I experimented with tiny vowel changes and endings, creating subtle distinctions without breaking the flow. I remembered the meticulous attention I had given to German compound words during my undergraduate studies. It was satisfying to create meaning with precision. This new language had that same elegance, yet in a musical form. Maybe I was feeling guilty about trying to own what was never mine to begin with.

I also decided sentence structure could be flexible too. I could arrange subject, verb, and object in a basic English-like order, but I could also highlight whichever part of the sentence mattered most. This echoed the topic–comment structures I had admired in Japanese and Korean.

My mind raced, comparing it to all the languages I had studied and learnt from other linguistic researchers. I let my body take over, scribbling symbols and sounds as if my hands knew the language before I did. Phonemes, tones, and patterns flowed onto the page in a dizzying rush, forming structures I hadn't consciously conceived.

It felt as if the grammar itself was guiding me, shaping sentences and contours that pulsed with meaning, urgent and alive beyond my control.

The city outside my Beacon Hill window sank into a hushed darkness, the kind that made every sound feel borrowed. One by one, the gas lamps flickered to life, amber glow spilling across the brick sidewalks.

Exhaustion tugged at my limbs, but my mind buzzed with excitement. I tried to anticipate meaning, like how a noun might shift in tone to signal different ideas, and how verbs could show time or intention through subtle changes of word particles.

I drew arrows between words, circled syllables, and scribbled little tone diagrams above them, even though my circles looked more like blobs than anything precise, but it didn't matter. The language felt alive, as if it were waiting to see how I would shape it.

Finally, as the night deepened, I let the melody of the language flood my mind completely.

The hypnotic tones, the rises, the falls, and the shifts, lulled me into sleep.

It was not ordinary sleep. It was a drifting, half-lucid state where dreams and grammar intertwined, and the language whispered in my head like it had its own consciousness.

△△△

By morning, my notebook was a tangle of scribbles, arrows, tone marks, and little sketches of word patterns. The pages were so crowded that I didn't even realize I had drawn some of them. There were a few that didn't even look like my handwriting. The strokes were sharper, almost frantic, as if written by a hand moving faster than my own. Some letters were slanted in ways I'd never written before, while others looped and curled into creative shapes I hadn't realized could still be read. I found myself staring at them, wondering what they'd meant when I jotted them down.

I ran my hands over my inflamed face and arms, feeling exhaustion, but also clarity and purpose.

This language wasn't just gibberish. No. It had internal consistency, logic, and beauty. I could almost hear it spoken aloud, not by one voice, but by a whole congregation from some ancient, forgotten civilization. Its rhythms rolled over consonants and vowels in ways that were hypnotic and deeply satisfying to my ears.

And then I knew it needed a name.

The language had brilliance, clarity, and an almost ethereal quality. It was like something radiant, untouchable, and powerful.

I thought about the way it had come to me, descending in melodies and harmonies that seemed to float in the mind like constellations in the sky. It was celestial, unique, and mesmerizing.

For some reason, the first word that came to me was Saraph.

It felt right.

Saraph—like *Seraph*, the winged, fiery beings of Hebrew mythology. It captured the melodic flow, the hypnotic rhythm, and the dangerous beauty of a language that was alive in my head.

It was as if the language had come from the heavens, from the sky itself.

Something about it was unmistakably special. Saraph was now officially a living language.

CHAPTER 10
FATED

A few days later, at exactly 1:56 a.m. on Thursday morning, my phone buzzed. At first, I thought it was another calendar reminder, or one of those spam texts about expiring subscriptions. It could've been a debt collector, or a notification from my brokerage account, which meant one of the automatic sell orders finally triggered after the stock hit its limit price.

But when I looked at the screen, my jaw dropped. The message came from an unsaved number.

No name, no country code. Just a plain, six-digit string of numbers.

You should have some ideas now. Take them.

I stared at it for a few seconds, half amused. But to be honest, I felt mostly uneasy.

It was like whoever sent it knew what I'd been doing, and what I'd been writing.

My notebook lay open beside me, filled with Saraph notes, phonetic transcriptions, syntactic trees, and interlinear glosses. The pages were slightly warped from the pressure of my hand tracing patterns deep into the night before.

The words on my phone's screen pulsed faintly under the dim light of my desk lamp.

I typed back: *Who is this?*

The reply came instantly.

Your soul mate.

I almost laughed and the sound caught in my throat.

I glanced around my apartment. I looked at the small lamp and listened to the quiet vibration of the heater.

Everything was normal. Too normal.

I replied again, fingers trembling slightly: *Stop messing with me.*

In a few seconds, I received a reply.

I'm your soul mate. I know who you are. I know what happened at the conference, in Sydney. I also know the whispers about the poisoned athlete, the chaos that no one ever connected to you. I know about your PhD, your work, the sleepless nights and the doubts you thought were only yours. I've been watching, learning, waiting.

I replied: *Who are you really?*

Nothing.

I waited.

The message didn't even show as 'delivered' anymore.

Then, after a few moments, the number vanished from the thread entirely.

One second, the message had been there, blinking insistently on the screen. The next, it was gone. Maybe it was a glitch. Maybe the phone provider had scrubbed it. Or maybe the sender was some prankster who'd found a way to hijack the Amber Alert system.

I stared at the empty screen, fingers hovering over the phone keyboard, my mind spinning through possibilities I couldn't quite grasp.

I checked my recent messages.

They were all gone.

It was like the messages I had just sent had never existed.

I copied and pasted the number into the dial pad, hit call and the automated voice cut in, "This number does not exist."

My mouth went dry.

I turned off my phone, and scanned my room.

The window blinds were half-open, revealing the usual slice of Beacon Hill's streets under the midnight glow. A streetlight flickered and then came a knocking sound. For a moment, I suddenly had the uncomfortable sense that someone could be watching me from one of the dark buildings across the street.

Maybe it was a stalker. Or an investigator, a journalist, a stranger who knew too much about what happened in Sydney.

Maybe it was no one, just a trick of reflection or light.

But once the thought surfaced, I couldn't shake it. A watcher could be anyone. It could be a janitor wiping down the steps of the State House, a tourist stumbling along the Freedom Trail, a neighbor pretending to adjust their blinds. They could record me, track my movements, trace the pattern of my walks, and build a story around the things I didn't say. All it would take was one photo, one glimpse at the wrong time, for everything to come undone.

But I reasoned with myself that at the same time, a quick google of my name would have shown everything. This would include the conference statement about the retracted journal that had been falsified, or the update on my PhD profile on MIT's website. Or even my date of birth, my relative names, and whether I'd been married.

My entire professional life was scattered across the internet, given the endless array of new social media websites, scraped databases and apps popping up these days, just waiting for someone with too much time and the wrong kind of curiosity to piece it all together.

I closed the blinds.

But even then, the unease wouldn't leave me. I paced the apartment, poured myself a glass of water, and tried to laugh it off. I opened the blinds, then closed them again. I checked the locks twice, then a third time, convinced they'd shifted when I wasn't looking. I turned on the radio, but between songs, the speakers hissed softly, like something alive was breathing in the wires.

I made tea just to fill the silence. The kettle's shriek felt too sharp like it was worried I wouldn't be able to hear it. I told myself I was safe. That the noise was ordinary. That walls didn't listen. But each lie came out thinner than the last, until the air itself seemed to wait for me to stop pretending.

"Maybe I've been overworking," I muttered, standing in the middle of the room, fingers tangled in my hair. "Maybe it's just spam. There's no stalker. Technology doesn't lie the way people do."

I grabbed my jacket and decided to walk it off. Maybe I could get some late-night clam chowder from The Harbor's Edge, two blocks down. Then I remembered I couldn't eat it because of my allergies, and I wasn't ready to break out in rashes again. Still, I figured they'd have a salad or something unprocessed. I would buy a bottle of water, if that's the only thing they had.

The cold Boston air slapped me awake as soon as I stepped outside. I pulled my hood up. I kept walking fast. The streets were almost empty, save for the occasional cab and the sound of my own footsteps.

My reflection flickered across the shop windows I passed. My image looked faint and slightly warped by the glass.

When I reached restaurant, the neon sign was off. The door was locked. Closed early.

"Great," I muttered under my breath.

Across the street, a 24/7 convenience store sat a few steps below street level, tucked into the block and bathed in the glow of a lone lamp. I crossed over and went inside, greeted by the faint buzz of the refrigerators and a bored cashier scrolling through his phone.

I grabbed a slice of banana bread. Something to chew on while pretending life was normal.

At the counter, I caught sight of myself in the store window. I thought it was just the glare from the overhead lights, but something was wrong. My reflection didn't look right. My pupils were too small. They looked like pinholes. They were tiny, black dots surrounded by a wide ring of pale iris.

I blinked hard, leaned closer, but the reflection blinked slower than I did, just half a second off.

My heart started pounding.

The cashier looked up at me, probably wondering why I was staring at the window like I'd seen a ghost.

"You okay, Jarvis?" he asked.

"How do you know my name?" I asked him.

He gave a short laugh. "You come here all the time, man," he said, scanning the barcode of my slice of banana bread. "You feeling okay? You haven't taken drugs or gotten food poisoning?"

I paid and stepped out quickly.

The cold air felt sharper now, and the sound of my shoes against the pavement echoed longer than it should have.

I yanked the hood tight until it bit into my temples, the world narrowing to a tunnel of shadow as I hurried back toward my apartment.

Halfway home, I threw the banana bread into a trash can outside.

I looked at my reflection in a parked car window.

My pupils were back to normal.

CHAPTER 11
SCARCITY

The next morning, my phone wouldn't stop ringing. The calls started when the light outside was just a thin wash of blue seeping through the blinds in nervous lines. The same number flashed again and again until I finally gave in and answered. My voice came out rough, frayed from a night spent half-sleeping, half-thinking.

"This is your bank calling," the representative said, his tone trained to sound calm, not kind. "We've noticed multiple failed withdrawal attempts for your rent payment submitted through your landlord's automated payment system."

I rubbed at my temple and tried to sound alert. "Right. That's fine. Just take whatever funds I have left in my account."

"That's not the issue, Mr. Lumen," he said flatly. "The problem is that the withdrawal amount has increased. According to the incoming request, your rent went up by an additional two thousand dollars this month. Have you checked with your landlord?"

For a second, the words didn't make sense.

I sat up, the blanket sliding to the floor. "Two thousand?" I asked. "Since when?"

"Apparently effective this month," he replied. "You may want to confirm whether they sent you any notice."

I frowned. "Wait—I should've gotten notice?"

"Yes, Mr. Lumen," he confirmed without hesitation. "And just to clarify, the new amount is tied to a renewed lease request that appears to be active in your landlord's system. I'd recommend reaching out to them directly before authorizing further payments."

"Really?" I asked, disbelief roughening my voice.

"Yes," he said again, half apologetically and half annoyed this time. "The increase was submitted through the property management portal earlier this week, and when the payment failed, the system automatically notified us."

I told him to sell some of my stocks. They were the last fragile illusion of a safety net I'd been holding onto. There was a pause, then the soft clicking of keys on his end.

"Mr. Lumen," he said after a moment, "have you seen the news? There's been a major market sell-off. Tech, biotech, even consumer stocks. Everything's dropped sharply overnight. Even if we execute your order, the proceeds won't cover your rent payment."

I sat still on the bed, watching my reflection blur in the window. Somewhere outside, a garbage truck scraped along Beacon Street, its engine growling like something chunky and ancient.

"I'm getting paid at the end of the week," I said quickly. "It'll be fine."

The silence that followed could be described as kindness or courtesy. Then came his measured voice again of someone reciting protocol rather than advice.

"Understood," he said. "But, Mr. Lumen, if I may offer a bit of free advice. You should take a careful look at your finances before making any large commitments. Your account's been under strain for some time now. If things continue this way, missed payments could seriously affect your credit standing and lead to potential legal action from creditors or your landlord. Just make sure you're not setting yourself up for something difficult to recover from."

The line clicked off.

I stayed there, staring at the black screen, the apartment around me filling faintly with morning light. The radiator rustled and popped in protest. The room smelled faintly of rotting food and something like vomit. I glanced at the unopened mail sitting on top of my drawer. The mountain of utility bills, credit card statements, and probably a letter of notice about the rent increase from my landlord, looked like Boston's version of a ticking time bomb.

The reality was simple: I didn't have enough. Not in my account, not in my head.

I knew there were more important things I should've been thinking about. For example, my candidacy presentation, Simeon's deadline. But at the same time, Vincent had already told me I'd be teaching additional subjects next semester, which would be enough to bring in a little extra income, at least until I finally graduated in two years' time and secured tenure… unless, of course, Simeon decided otherwise.

And if things went bad—really bad—there was always the quiet, unspoken backup plan of moving back in with my parents. Even by then, I'd be thirty-five. Too old for it, too proud for it, but not too broke. I'd keep my head down, unpack quietly, and pretend it was temporary. I'll convince myself that it wasn't failure, just transition. No one had to know. It would just be another dirty secret folded into the rest to never admit out loud, except in the silence that comes before sleep.

It felt like my brain was splitting into two incompatible halves. One was muttering about my passion for syntax and linguistic models. The other was whispering human survival. Which bill could wait? Which card had room left? Which lie could stretch a little longer before tearing completely?

I pressed my forehead against the cold windowpane. The city outside looked calm in the early light of sunrise as employees headed to their workplaces. Taxis idled at the curb. Students in thick coats trudged toward the T station. I watched someone drop an envelope stamped '*OVERDUE*' and keep walking. No one stopped to pick it up. Then I looked closer—and realized the person was me.

CHAPTER 12
INVITATION

The whole of the next week was brutal. From early Monday morning to Thursday afternoon, every day felt like a test of endurance. I spent hours grading student work—syntax exercises, phonetics assignments, essays on language evolution—while trying to balance my own research, teaching responsibilities, and Simeon's looming deadline for my candidacy presentation, which had somehow shrunk into two weeks.

Between emails and drafts, I caught myself calculating rent in my head, thinking about what I could sell to make up the difference. Something that wouldn't drain more time, something I could let go of without losing more of myself. Old clothes? Old electronics? My soul? Each thought felt a little more desperate, a little more realistic.

Each paper I graded reminded me that time was slipping away. That the pressure to justify my PhD, to prove I wasn't wasting my efforts on fantasy, was relentless. I'd skipped meals, not just to save time but to save money, convincing myself that every sacrifice would somehow make the work mean more.

On Tuesday morning, Simeon showed up at my office without warning. He leaned against the doorframe, arms folded, watching me with that patient, managerial smile that always meant trouble.

"I've been emailing you," he said in his unmistakable posh accent. His nostrils flared with each breath. "Several times, actually. No reply. Or are you just choosing which messages to answer these days?"

Before I could explain that I'd only been following Vincent's advice—not to ignore Simeon, but to limit communication so I wouldn't get sidetracked—he forced himself into the room and set an empty folder on my desk with deliberate care. It felt like an invasion of personal space.

"Make a copy of everything you've done so far," he said, his eyes drifting over the clutter like he was cataloguing the wreckage of my concentration. "All drafts, notes, transcripts. I want to see your progress."

In the afternoon, he came back into my office. He told me I was now required to attend several first-year

PhD presentations "for perspective," as he put it. The first one was scheduled for Friday morning at 11 a.m., in the lecture hall downstairs.

Then, on Wednesday in the late afternoon, he appeared again—unannounced, of course—the way deans do when they want to remind you that your time doesn't belong to you. He leaned on the doorframe, his thin smile barely concealing irritation. A vein was visibly standing out on his right temple.

"I don't know what Vincent's been telling you," he said, his voice rougher than the last time he spoke to me. "Or if it was him who told you to ignore my emails *again*. But I'd prefer you listen to me, Jarvis, because I'm the dean, and I outrank him."

I blinked, unsure whether he expected an answer. But I knew, for my own sake, I should keep quiet.

"You're working on something… unconventional, and I guess Vincent doesn't want me to get in the way," he went on, his fingers tapping hard against the doorframe. "That's fine, in theory. But understand, I have the Provost, the Department Chair, and the Research Oversight Committee to answer to. They don't respond well to research that looks like mythology. If you want your candidacy to stand a chance, you'll do exactly as I say. Less improvisation. More structure. Because right now, you are currently inefficient."

The final word landed harder than it should have. I swallowed the bitterness gathering behind my teeth at the sound of 'inefficient.'

The last time someone had described me that way was back in my freshman year, by a professor who didn't even bother to look up from his attendance sheet. He told me it was my responsibility to fix my own enrollment issues, that an administrative delay wasn't an excuse for a late assignment. Then he lazily branded me *inefficient.* Hearing it when I was still getting used to college life, back when I was naïve enough to believe authority always meant guidance, lodged the word deeper than it had any right to, and the wound had never really healed.

"Understood," I said quietly.

He nodded once, already looking past me at the papers scattered on my desk. "You can start by spending less time at lunch," he continued, turning around to leave. "I've seen you walking around campus in the afternoons, muttering to yourself. You could use that time more efficiently."

I just stared at the back of his head and his ruffled hair tangled in sweat. I was too drained to argue. I hadn't even eaten lunch. Maybe he thought I'd been wasting time chatting with other PhD candidates, when in reality, I'd been asking if I could borrow a little money to cover my debt so I could actually focus on my research for once, instead of panicking about rent.

When Simeon finally went, the silence he left behind felt heavier than before.

Memories of the humiliation at the conference in Sydney began to resurface. The goggling eyes, frozen faces, whispers of failure reflected back at me in every mirrored surface I passed. Then there was the death of that athlete. The paranoia never left. Every reflection on every window, spoon, metal chairs felt like it could hide those pinhole pupils again.

I was certain I hadn't lost my mind.

My shoulders ached from hunching over all the assignments and notes. But at least my notes on my invented Saraph language continued to grow, whether or not Simeon could see it. They sat beside my desk, fragments of a tonal language forming in my mind, waiting for me to give them life. Every scribble—though my drawings were nothing short of terrible—felt like proof that I could still build something real, something that might outlast the humiliation and exhaustion that had broken me.

Then Vincent's email appeared in my inbox. It was sandwiched between a reminder about course evaluations and three increasingly curt messages from my landlord warning that rent was officially past due.

I stared at the subject line: Bus Leaves in a Few Hours.

The message was short but urgent:

Jarvis, there is a group of screenwriters and movie fans in New York City who meet weekly at Hotel Hawthorne. They've been inventing languages together for decades. You need to go. Observe, record, immerse yourself. I've arranged a bus to get you there in a few hours. Trust me. This is important. Do not miss it! Bus ticket is attached.

– Vincent

P.S. And Jarvis—don't listen to Simeon or do anything he asks for now. I'll speak with him later and straighten things out. For the moment, stay focused on this assignment.

If Vincent had gone as far as to purchase a bus ticket for me, it had to be serious. He wasn't the kind of person to act on impulse. Whatever was happening at this meeting tonight, it had to matter.

I barely had time to grab anything besides my recorder and notebook. I didn't even go back to my apartment to prepare a meal I could eat on the way since I couldn't eat out due to my allergies. There was no time, no reason, and it would've been inefficient. I just took a bottle of water Vincent had conveniently left in the kitchen, knowing it was the only thing I ever drank.

Maybe there was a visiting academic that carried real weight in the field, or perhaps the meeting was centered on a topic directly tied to my research. Either way, it had to mean something.

I left my office at MIT, the graded papers and Saraph's phonetic charts and tonal transcriptions stacked on my desk, and headed to Copley Square, close to Downtown Boston, where Vincent had arranged the bus to Manhattan. Behind all the urgency and uncertainty, I reminded myself to breathe, to have faith that Vincent knew what he was doing, that he had everything about me under control.

△△△

The I-95 highway stretched endlessly ahead as the bus rumbled south toward New York City. Behind me, Boston's brick streets and the glimmer of the Charles River receded, giving way to the blur of roadside diners, gas stations, and the rhythm of the highway beneath the fading light of dusk.

My mind spun with anticipation and exhaustion, drifting between fleeting thoughts of what I might encounter at the language meetup in Hotel Hawthorne. I wondered whether I'd meet someone who could challenge my understanding, uncover a new linguistic pattern, or witness a conversation so precise it would reshape the way I thought about language itself.

As the bus neared Manhattan, the skyline rose like blocks of crystals.

Times Square's neon chaos flickered through the bus windows like a riot of colors, motion, and sound, advertising Broadway musicals, pizza places, and late-night souvenir shops. It made my chest tighten with both awe and fatigue.

When the bus finally arrived, most of the passengers had rushed to one of the food stalls for a late, desperate dinner. But I, on the other hand, ran through the crowd straight towards Hotel Hawthorne. Making a strong impression could help open doors and connections that might one day prove invaluable for my PhD and the work that would follow.

The hotel was large, though not as vast as the Marriott Marquis in Times Square, from the direction I had just come. But still, it was grand enough to house ballrooms and boardrooms often rented for weddings and corporate events. As I approached Hotel Hawthorne, I could see why similar meet-ups and events could easily take place there.

The hotel's neon sign flickered faintly on the rooftop, half-inviting, half-mysterious, as if it had been waiting for me all along. I pushed past a guest that was wheeling a suitcase, their eyes buried in the latest Playbill magazine featuring the current Broadway musicals.

The bellman standing by the entrance, bundled in a thick coat, raised an eyebrow.

"Evening," I said. "I was told there's a language group that meets here on Friday nights?"

The bellman glanced at me, tilting his head. Something passed across his expression. Was it unease? Did he think I was someone else?

"What language meetup?" he asked quietly.

"Isn't there a language meetup that happens here every week?"

"We have many meetups and even conventions happening in Hotel Hawthorne all the time," he said. "Unless there is a very specific one you have in mind."

The bellman stepped inside the lobby, motioning with one hand for me to wait by the door. He adjusted his cuffs, glanced briefly toward the reception desk, then disappeared behind a mirrored column. There was the faint rustle of keys, drawers, and maybe whispers. Finally, he reappeared, his expression uneasy.

"Look… the manager's your person," he said, nodding toward the counter, his lips drawn thin, eyes fixed on the floor. "Something about this doesn't feel right. They'll decide if you can go in."

I nodded, trying to mask my nerves, and followed him into the lobby. The chandeliers cast a dim yellow light across polished floors, having long lost their original shine.

The manager, a woman with hair tightly coiled into a bun, looked up and stepped out from behind the front desk to stand beside me. Her arms crossed lightly over her chest and her shoulders were squared; feet planted firmly. She shifted her weight slightly toward me. I was done trying to assert control. Some people owned the room the second they stood still.

"I'm here about the language group," I said.

"Sorry, I think you got the wrong hotel," she replied without hesitation.

"This is Hotel Hawthorne, right?"

The manager's lips curved faintly as her gaze drifted toward the grand hotel logo, featuring interlocking wings, emblazoned on the wall behind the long marble counter.

"This is Hotel Hawthorne, right on one of the busiest streets in all of New York City," she confirmed. "But the group you mentioned that started here decades ago has been gone for as long as I can remember. There haven't been any official meetings in years, so I'm confused why you're here. People like you still come sometimes, hoping to find something that isn't here anymore. But I think you should probably leave."

But Vincent told me to come. He even booked a bus for me. It has to be real. Could there be some mistake? Either that, or the staff doesn't know the full story.

"History's complicated," she continued, as though she had read my mind. "And frankly, I don't want to talk about it anymore. Not to you, not to any journalists or whatever it is you do. You've asked too many questions."

"I'm a linguist," I said to her, watching the bellman greet new guests and direct them toward the correct elevators. "Perhaps you're thinking about the wrong group?"

Her voice hardened. "If you don't leave on your own, I'll have security escort you out. And if that doesn't work, I won't hesitate to call the NYPD myself. This isn't a game. I don't know who you are, you don't have a reservation, and frankly, I don't care. You're making things difficult, and I've got better things to do than explain decades-old nonsense to some stranger."

The manager slid back behind the counter and leaned slightly, her gaze piercing. "Do you understand? I suggest you turn around before this gets ugly. If you're so eager to record or study languages, the street outside is full of different voices, accents and dialects from across the world. Go collect all the linguistic diversity you want out there, and leave this hotel out of it."

I paused, taking in the polished floors and dim chandeliers, imagining the faint echoes of voices from meetings that had supposedly taken place here decades ago. I wondered if she expected me to apologize and admit I was intruding, even though I knew the whole thing was just a misunderstanding.

As I turned to leave, I foolishly expected the doorman to open the glass door. But he did not. I walked straight into the door, and I barely caught myself before hitting my head.

CHAPTER 13
CONTACT

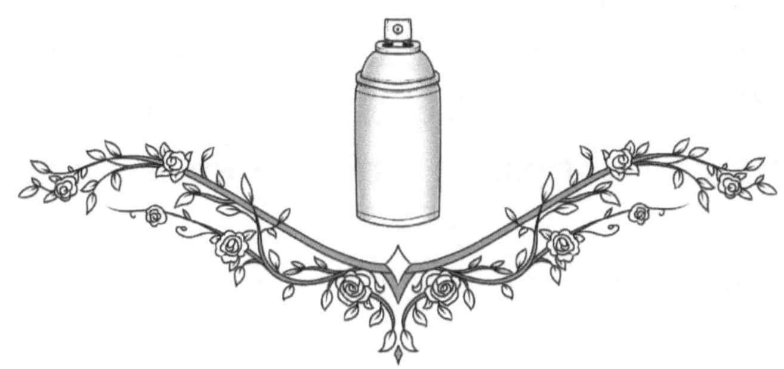

I stepped outside, the fractured glow of Hotel Hawthorne flickering behind me. The street was alive with honking cars, distant chatter and sirens. Like the manager said, they were the very sound that proved you were in New York. Voices in countless languages and accents spilled around me.

Then an itch started crawling across my forearms.

And that's when I heard the faint, metallic hiss of spray paint.

The sound was recurring and exact, echoing through a narrow alleyway I hadn't noticed before, just a few steps away. It was tucked between two shadowed brick buildings, cluttered with overflowing dumpsters and streaked with layers of fresh graffiti.

My eyes scanned the sidewalk, and there he was, standing in the alleyway beneath the pale glow of a flickering streetlamp. His rough coat hung off him in uneven folds, thinned and stained from weather and time. I thought it looked like the kind of garment that had long stopped keeping anyone warm. His shoes were mismatched, his jeans torn at the knees.

Paint cans lay scattered at his feet like abandoned shells. When I looked deeper into the alley, I saw the walls were not just painted, but smothered by a mural of faces.

The man holding the paint can had skin that gleamed in the lamplight, painted with streaks that looked like sweat, or maybe blood.

"Hey," he called, looking up sharply the moment he realized I'd been staring. "You recording me or something? What's your name?"

"I'm… Jarvis," I managed, the words catching in my throat. "And you are?"

He straightened, flicking paint from his fingers. "Oakley," he said, brushing streaks from his palms. "You here for that event in Hotel Hawthorne?"

"You mean the meetup?" I said, swallowing hard. "I'm a linguist, a PhD researcher. I heard there was a long-running screenwriters' group here. The kind where they build new languages from scratch or something. I came hoping to learn from them, but the hotel staff told me——"

"Learn?" Oakley cut me off with a short, dry laugh. He stepped back, eyeing me as if measuring how clueless I was. "You really think you can walk in, study them, and stroll back out?"

"I just—"

"No," he snapped, and looked away. "Take my advice. People who come looking for that group don't leave with notes or goodie bags. They don't leave at all."

"They disappear?"

Oakley's expression darkened. Without warning, he stepped over, grabbed my wrist and yanked me into the narrow strip of shadow with him. "Quiet," he hissed.

He glanced up and around, scanning the windows of the hotel, the dumpsters, the rooftops. His breathing tightened, as if he expected someone to be watching.

Only then when the wind slowed down, did he speak again, his voice barely above a whisper.

"Ever wonder why the hotel never lets anyone near that meetup, or why they don't even pull out their guest logs?" His grip loosened but didn't let go. "Once a budding actor from North Carolina came through. Bright kid, like you. He was apparently invited to the meeting." He paused, eyes flicking back toward the hotel. "He vanished afterward. Been missing for over a year now. No leads. No body." He shook the paint can in his hand. "But trust me… he's dead."

"Are you sure?"

"I'm telling you," Oakley said, jaw tightening until the muscles stood out under his skin. His voice dropped into something harsh and strained, as if the words were being dragged out of him. "Everyone who hunts for that meetup, or even knows too much about it, dies."

"But you know plenty," I said quietly, the words coming out sharper than I intended. "And you're standing here."

"I survive because I watch," Oakley growled, voice rough but urgent. "I stay on the street. I keep my distance. Curious people like you show up every few months. They poke around for a night or two, trying to get answers." He flicked his fingers like wings, mimicking something vanishing. "It'll be your turn to be gone. No checks, no calls, no bodies. And nobody ever speaks about it again."

Oakley glared at me, his eyes sharp and furious. His arms looked as tense as springs.

"If you push too far, you won't like what you find," he said, warning me again. "You're lucky I'm even talking to you, warning you. My advice to you is to forget about this meetup and go back doing whatever you were doing, and don't expect anyone to explain themselves. You'll regret it."

Oakley turned, crouching low once more, and continued spraying the wall, each new stroke forcing the painted faces to stare with even more intensity. I got a feeling he didn't want to hurt me. If anything, he seemed concerned I'd see what he was really painting.

I wanted to ask him more questions so I could discover the truth, but he was the third person to warn me off, after the bellman and the manager at Hotel Hawthorne.

My hands shook, a cold certainty settling over me that he had nothing more to say. And yet, I couldn't bring myself to turn and leave because that would make me—as Simeon said—inefficient.

CHAPTER 14

BIRTHDAY

"Y ou've got to tell me what you know about this language meet up," I pleaded to Oakley. "I know my professor from MIT wouldn't have sent me here for nothing."

Oakley eyed met mine, warily. "I'll give you credit for being so brave that you want to know more," he said. "I take it you don't have a wife or girl to go back home to."

"It's not that," I replied, forcing a small smile as I stepped a little closer, palms open at my sides. "It took me almost five hours to get here, and I have other people that depend on me to know more about this meetup."

He sighed, and his voice became low and sharp.

"Look, I don't show this to anyone and most people prefer not to know," he said. "Not without… payment…"

Of course, Oakley was homeless, otherwise he wouldn't be crouched here in this alley, spray can in hand, surrounded by his chaotic gallery of faces. He had probably tried everything once. Shelters had thrown him out for breaking curfew. Jobs fired him for breaking protocol. Rehab programs that mistook silence for progress.

And yet, a part of me wondered what desperation or pride had driven him to demand something in return for sharing what he know about this meetup.

He crossed his arms and shook his head. "I'm unemployed, man. I don't even have a place to call home. No wife, no kid, no one waiting for me if I get cold at night. Just me and whatever's left in my pockets."

What could I give him? The only cash I had were a few gold coins from Australia. There was no way he could accept electronic payments like credit cards.

And then I remembered the small package of vegan chocolate Jolin had given me back in Sydney.

I pulled the beautifully wrapped chocolate out, holding it uncertainly. "Will this work?"

Oakley's eyes lit up briefly, just enough for me to see he was hungry, before he said, "A piece of chocolate? C'mon, you've got to have something more valuable than that. I'm not a kid no more. But you know what, I'm starving and I wouldn't mind a short sugar rush. I guess that'll do this time. Just this time."

He snatched the chocolate from my hand and tore into it right there, taking a quick large bite, like he was afraid it'd be taken away. Crumbs clung to his fingers as he leaned closer toward me, lowering his voice. "We're going through the back staircase. No one's allowed there. If we stay longer than two minutes, the alarm will go off. You don't want that."

"Got it."

Without another word, he led me around the side of the hotel, past the polished front entrance I had just left, to a narrow, rusted fire escape tucked into the shadows beside a forgotten service door.

The metal steps groaned under our weight as we climbed, making me question my sanity for trusting someone homeless. What if this was a cruel prank? The distant noise of the city was muted by the surrounding brick walls, pressing in around us. I didn't know why, but the place had an energy that quickened my blood.

"We have to move fast," Oakley warned, glancing up the stairs. "Two minutes. That's all you get."

We climbed quickly. The cold metal railing bit at my palms. My legs burned. My heart pounded, but we both moved with surprising speed, almost like we had memorized every step, every turn.

Finally, we reached the rooftop.

The roof itself was wide and uneven, a patchwork of concrete and rusted vents humming with trapped heat. A single water tower loomed in the corner with its shadow stretching long and thin. The hotel's neon sign buzzed faintly beside it with an appealing carnival glow, half the letters burned out, casting a trembling light across the gravel.

From the edge of the rooftop's railing, I could see Manhattan stretching out beneath us. Lights shimmered from Times Square down Broadway and Seventh Avenue, spilling over the bridges and tracing the curve of the Hudson. The city glowed like a living constellation. From this height, the whole island looked like a toy model set gently aglow by the hands of something divine.

And there, sprawling across the asphalt and sidewalks below, were the murals, where me and Oakley had just recently met. From this new angle, the neon lights of Times Square and the glowing windows of nearby towers cast shifting colors and reflections across the painted walls below, turning the murals into something of a living canvas of stories.

"These are the people," Oakley was the first to break the silence, speaking around a mouthful of chocolate. The bar was bitten down to a ragged edge, melting between his fingers. "The ones who came here… met here… and died."

I could see it now. There were hundreds of faces, smeared in every color of the rainbow. Eyes were stretched too wide. Mouths twisted into crooked screams. Noses collapsed inwards. They reminded me of lowbrow surrealism, a type of art movement from the late 70s and 80s that depicted disturbing subjects drawn in bright cartoon. But something about the sight clawed at my nerves. I could not place what it was at first. I knew for a fact it was not their genders, or their races, or even their expressions.

And when the realization eventually settled in, it came with a cold and quiet shock. Not a single face in the murals belonged to anyone past middle age. It was as if the mural itself was intentionally painted to refuse acknowledgment of anyone who had lived long enough to understand what was coming. I wondered if it was meant to symbolize something darker, or if it was chosen the same way funerals tend to use young photographs, focusing only on the sanitized, untroubled version of a person.

"Died?" I swallowed hard, turning toward the edge of the roof. "How?"

Oakley shrugged. He wiped at his cheek, smudging it with a mix of chocolate and dried red paint. "No one knows for sure. The police and journalists tried to investigate, but nothing was ever publicized. Some drowned in places no one would think to search. Others had drills buried in their skulls. And some simply vanished. I've spent years trying to make sense of it. And as I painted these lost souls, something strange happened. My own illnesses began to heal."

"You must've discovered something they all had in common," I said, my voice faltering.

Oakley's eyes sharpened, and he looked at me up and down.

"How old are you?" he asked me.

"Thirty-three," I said, cautiously.

He nodded slowly. "Born April 28, 1992?"

My brain short-circuited. "Yes… how do you–"

"They were all born then too," he said quietly, his voice thinning as he turned back to the mural, eyes heavy as if it had just reminded him of something he wished he could forget. "Every single one of them. Same age. Same birthday."

And same astrological signs too? I wanted to say.

"I don't know why," he continued, whispering now. "It's not a coincidence, I tell you. I don't know what it means. But it's the pattern I see. Every single victim had been born on the same date. Of course I haven't painted every single victim, but I am sure the evidence is already clear. I paint them, I remember them, I survive. That's all I know."

"Do you think I could be next then?" I turned to face him, urgency in my voice.

"Maybe," he said softly, turning to me, eyeing me strangely. "Unless you've got someone riding with you, who's willing to stand by you, someone who actually wants to share their life with you and look out for you. Then maybe you've got a shot. But if you're on your own… if you're just a solo man like me, then it's only God calling the shots."

I frowned, curiosity pushing through the unease. "But… why do you paint them at all? All these people who died?"

Oakley lifted one shoulder, slipping the empty chocolate wrapper into the pocket of his paint-streaked pants. "It's like people painting Jesus, or Mary, or whatever god you believe in. It calms them. It calms me. It's ritual, I guess. A way to honor them, remember them, and it gives me purpose."

I stared down at the murals, at the frozen expressions.

The eyes seem to follow me even from the rooftop. The thought of all those people sharing some strange cosmic alignment, and then dying, made my stomach churn. That meant I had no escape from it.

I was next.

And yet, part of me couldn't look away.

"You want to see more?" Oakley stepped back, folding his arms and smiling cheekily. "You want to know what happens next? Come back tomorrow, but you'll need to pay me again. And it won't be cheap next time."

CHAPTER 15

NEGLIGENCE

As soon as I left the hotel and Oakley, I stumbled into the streets. My heart hammered so violently I felt like it might burst. The city blurred around me with lights streaking past, car horns blaring, footsteps echoing.

But none of it registered.

All I could think about was survival.

I could be next to die.

I should have listened to the doorman and the manager at Hotel Hawthorne and gone away. Maybe they were trying to warn me without being mocked.

But then again, maybe Oakley was just playing with me. This was how he made his money. He lured people in, tempted them with a glimpse of a mysterious conspiracy, and then asked for more payment each time, never letting them leave satisfied. And somehow, he'd managed to get me too. I wanted to believe I was different, that I saw through his tricks.

That's when I realized I hadn't even booked a proper hotel yet.

My original plan had been to return to Boston on a sleeper bus. But everything felt wrong in such a climactic moment. There was definitely no way I was going to spend another five hours on a bus empty-handed with nothing to add to my research. I didn't want Simeon to tell me I was inefficient again. I wasn't going to enforce some arbitrary schedule when the work still felt unfinished.

After wandering several blocks, past the tribal house mix of some gay nightclubs in Hell's Kitchen and the distant chatter of late-night crowds, I saw a small, slightly run-down hostel tucked between two taller buildings.

The neon sign outside of the hotel flickered faintly: *Skyline Hostel – Private Rooms Available.*

I didn't even know if it was a safe part of the city. Frankly, I didn't care. The hostel was indeed random. But it seemed affordable. And it promised privacy.

I pushed through the door into the hostel, the cheap bell jingling.

A young man behind the counter barely looked up. His hair was messy in a way that looked unintentional, like he'd run his hands through it one too many times.

"Room for the night?" I asked, trying to steady my voice.

"Private or dorm?" he said, raising an eyebrow as a small stud glinted in his ear.

"I need privacy," I said, my hands trembling.

"That'll be $30," he replied. "ID?"

I fumbled through my bag, finally pulling out my faded license, in which he handed me a keycard with a short warning. The key felt heavy in my hand like a talisman.

"Room 13," he said, without meeting my gaze. "Quiet hours, don't cause trouble, and don't try anything weird. Break the rules, you're out. You look mature, so I trust you."

I pushed down the narrow hallway, the neon from the street outside flickering across the walls. The paint was chipped, the air thick with damp linen and old smoke. Doors lined each side, some cracked open, some sealed tight, the numbers barely hanging on.

My mind raced with Oakley's words, the murals, the mysterious deaths.

Was it really possible? I was having second, third and fourth thoughts now.

Room 13 was small but private, and should I also mention, hard to open. On one side was a narrow bed pushed against the wall. Right beside it sat a desk with one of its legs banded in place with scotch tape, a kettle perched on top beside a few packets of instant coffee and tea, along with a handful of worn paperbacks left by previous guests. Overhead, a flickering lamp buzzed weakly. The en-suite bathroom was barely more than a closet with a showerhead, its tiles cold and mismatched, the mirror warped at the edges.

I dropped my bag and sank onto the mattress, wrapping the thin blanket around me like a shield. I didn't want to shower. I wasn't in the mood to call Vincent and explain to him what I had just discovered. I wasn't even going to get dinner. It would've been a waste of time and energy.

△△△

Around 2:15 a.m., my phone buzzed.

The number was unfamiliar.

I answered hesitantly.

A rough, distorted voice came through.

"Yeah… it's me," Oakley rasped, and I immediately recognized the uneven cadence of someone hardened by life on the streets. "From a payphone… and I only put a dollar in, so let me talk," he added, almost as an afterthought, each word dragging like it cost him more than the last.

My stomach dropped. "Oakley, what's happening?"

"The hell… you even can ask me that question," he said, his voice strangled, choking on each word. "How could you, man?"

Every syllable was jagged, broken by violent coughs and ragged wheezes. His voice shook and cracked, occasionally disappearing into a wet, gurgling rasp that sent a cold spike of acid down my spine. Even for someone without any trained medical background, I could tell he was struggling.

"Are you okay?" I asked.

"Do you really think I would be okay after being poisoned?" Oakley replied painfully. "I can feel it burning. My skin's getting cold. My veins feel thick."

"What are you talking about?" I said, my pulse quickening. "Do you need me to call you an ambulance?"

"By the time the ambulance comes, I'll be dead," he croaked, coughing. "That was your plan all along, wasn't it? So, you don't just survive. You also make someone else pay for it. You think calling anyone will help now? You did this. You and your people from your cult."

"Cult?" I replied. My voice cracked, more defensive than I meant it to be. "I already told you everything I am."

The line rattled with his strained breath, leaving the rest of his words suspended, choking inside the telephone booth. For a while, I thought the sound was static, but it was actually him fighting for air until all there was left was the hiss of dying breath and the wet, broken gasp of someone who knew they weren't going to make it.

Then a heavy silence like the night itself had closed over his body.

I sank against the wall, blanket clutched around me.

My skin itched; my heartrate thundered.

I could feel something shifting inside me again.

Oakley was gone. It was irreversible.

And yet, as the silence stretched, I couldn't stop the questions from spiraling. *Could I really have poisoned him?* The chocolate. It had come from Jolin. She would never do such a thing. She was on my side. I've known her for years. She even asked if I liked it and asked if I wanted more.

Then there was the athlete, poisoned with the water.

This was the second death I had caused. Whether directly or indirectly, I still caused the death.

Was it really a coincidence, or was something far stranger going on?

My careful calculations, my sleepless nights, the hours spent shaping language hadn't prepared me for this. I wondered, with a chill I couldn't shake, whether the scholar I thought I was even existed anymore.

But then I felt a vibration coming from my pocket. I fished out my phone with trembling fingers. The screen lit up my face in a sickly glow. Someone had just sent me a text message. The timing was precise, as if whoever it was had been waiting for the moment my guard finally slipped to contact me.

It was a text from the mysterious number again.

CHAPTER 16
PROPHECY

The number on my phone was again from an unknown sender. Hesitating for a moment, I tapped the screen and opened the text. I stared at the screen until the cryptic words began to blur. Were they silently implying that I was indeed responsible for the murders?

I know you're feeling lost. Because I am too. After all I'm your soul mate. Taking a life for something greater isn't murder. It's purpose. If you just listen to your recording, you might find the answer.

My throat felt dry, like I'd swallowed sand.

And then there was the title they used. *Soul mate.*

It was same phrase from that night that vanished as soon as I replied.

I typed back: *What recording?*

The three dots appeared for a moment, then vanished.

No reply.

A drafty wind slipped through the cracked window.

I stood, every nerve on edge, straining to catch any movement in the shadows of the room.

Above me, I noticed the ceiling was stained with water. The door was hung half-open by half an inch. Somewhere down the hall, a television hummed with a sharp sound of another guest in the otherwise, unmoving air.

When I was growing up, my mother always told me to listen to the air, the walls, the pauses between sounds. She didn't mean it literally, of course. But I understood she was telling me to pay attention to the things most people ignore, such as the quiet warnings the world gives off before something awful happens. So, I listened harder. I let the silence press against my ears. I searched for the faintest intake of breath, a floorboard settling, and even the movements of something that shouldn't.

Then something clattered.

My recorder fell to the floor, its red light blinking faintly. I bent down, picking it up by the cracked edge.

The recorder wasn't some cheap pocket device. It was one of those professional field recorders linguists take on research trips. The university had loaned me it so I could capture every nuance and shift of a voice in uncompressed format. The metal casing was more dented than my phone, but it was still *intact*, still functional in that stubborn, almost indestructible way academic equipment tends to be. For a split second, the surface reflected something behind me.

There was someone.

A face, pale and too close.

Teeth so small they looked carved down, filed smooth like bone.

Eyes unblinking.

I jerked around.

The window curtains fluttered.

But there was no one. Just the outline of my own reflection, stretched thin against the window glass.

And beneath the sounds of the nightclubs, I swore I heard something else. It was my own voice, whispering faintly from the recorder, playing back words I didn't remember saying.

CHAPTER 17
TAPPED

The red light on the recorder blinked, steady and alive, and I pressed play again. A hiss bloomed from the device. It was a sickly exhale of grainy static that rose and fell like waves gnawing against metal hulls. I'd used this model more times than I could count, and had even coached new linguists through their first recordings. Of all those times, it had never produced a sound like this.

Then something totally unexpected dragged-out. It was my own slow voice crackling through. I sounded as though I were speaking from underwater.

But the strangest part was that the language spilling out wasn't English.

It wasn't anything that should have come from my throat.

Its rhythm pulsed in impossible tonal climbs and drops, almost like a warped Chinese dialect. But it was too fluid. Every syllable was a sound and a breath that pushed through me. Consonants melted like wax into voiceless fricatives that slid into velar hums, vowels stretched beyond what living lungs could exhale. Triplet tones sharpened in ways no human vocal cords should achieve.

There was a melody behind it.

A hymn, laced with grit and teeth.

Saraph.

The language I'd been building from real endangered languages and half-lucid thoughts.

Except this wasn't my version.

For a moment I forgot it was my voice at all. It could have belonged to any male.

Then came another sound.

Metal.

A hollow clang.

Followed by water dripping in slow, deliberate rhythm.

I knew that sound because visions of it flashed back. It belonged on the roof of the Hotel Hawthorne, exactly where Oakley and I had stood last night. Where he'd explained the people he painted in his murals were people that had vanished.

Had I somehow gone back up there? Had I been dragged there against my consent? My head throbbed as if echoing an impact, but there was no memory of it.

The mumbling on the tape grew louder.

Other faint echoes surfaced beneath mine. Then they sharpened like silhouettes out of a fog. The voices shot upward by nearly two octaves without a single break, without breath, without the slightest shift in register. It was as if the sound itself had forgotten it needed a body to make it.

I remembered the day vocal registers were covered in my undergraduate phonetics class. Our professor had stood at the front of a dim lecture hall beside a spectrogram diagram, explaining that humans cannot glide their voice perfectly smoothly across more than one and a half to two octaves without a break, a breath, or a shift in register. He had even invited students to try to prove him wrong.

The room had briefly sounded like a hilarious chorus of failed *American Idol* hopefuls. But the point was, no matter how many attempts were made, no one came close. And now, whenever I hear something rise far beyond what a human throat should manage, I'm reminded that what I'm hearing should be impossible. Or least, it wasn't being vocalized by one person.

The dozens of voices coming out of the recorder in my hand bought me back to the present. They were the sounds of men and women. Their tones layered perfectly in the same strange melody, warping high and low, speaking the same tongue I supposedly invented. Some whispered in rasping breaths. Others murmured in perfect unison with my cadence, as though I hadn't been speaking alone but had joined a ritual already in motion.

I turned the volume up, pressing the recorder to my ear even as dread pressed harder into my ribs.

The voices were harmonizing with me.

Then, right before the tape clicked off, something new slipped through.

It was a whisper so faint it was like a vibration more than a sound.

And it wasn't in Saraph.

It was English.

"You heard us," the voice said.

The recorder slipped from my hands before I realized I'd moved. It hit the floor hard, spinning once, the red light still blinking like an exposed pulse.

CHAPTER 18
DEBUNKED

By dawn, I couldn't tell what was dream, what was fiction, and what was memory anymore. Honking taxis, shouting pedestrians, and the endless sounds of food vendors from outside disrupted by thoughts. The recorder was on the desk. Its red light was dead now, but my head kept replaying the sounds and the terrible memories I didn't remember living. They were things I was certain had never happened.

The voices.

The dripping water.

The whisper that said "you heard us."

However, after a few hours of quality sleep, though not merely enough, it all tangled together. The meeting in Hotel Hawthorne that never existed, Oakley's haunted eyes, his murals of dead strangers who shared my birthday, the Sydney conference, the poisoned athlete, the texts from a 'soul mate' who also didn't exist. Most importantly, being accused of being inefficient. There's something very engaging about patterns that shouldn't exist—and the way your mind insists they do.

Every thought folded into another until I couldn't tell which version of me was real. Was it the one running from Beacon Hill to MIT in 10 minutes? Or the one trapped behind glass reflections?

When the alarm on my phone went off at its usual time, my skin started to burn again.

It began with an itch behind my ears, then crawled down my neck, spreading across my shoulders like fire ants. I scratched until my nails came away dotted with flakes. My arms looked raw and were patterned with angry red streaks.

I tried to rationalize it.

Stress.

Sleep deprivation.

Maybe my body was just catching up to the chaos.

But then a thought slipped in.

That night in the business lounge, before the Sydney flight, my skin had been almost perfect when I woke up. The only difference then was the room's humidity. I'd fallen asleep with the shower mist still clinging to the air, warm and damp like a cloud around me. I even remember Brendan telling me in a half witty and half teasing tone to turn off the shower the next time I slept, as if he expected I might wander back there someday and he would be around to remind me again.

Maybe that was it. Moisture. Humidity. A simple, logical explanation. Science. Not curses. Not astrology.

I remember my dermatologist telling me that skin only heals when the barrier stays moist. Humidity softens the surface and lets micro-tears close. At the same time, dry air pulls moisture out and turns every tiny irritation into something the body treats like a wound. That was why petroleum jelly helped so much because it trapped water and gave my skin a seal to repair itself. It also explained why the last time I was in Miami, the heavy coastal air felt like a natural balm. But at Denver, the thin, dry altitude made my skin tighten by afternoon.

So I decided to test the theory.

I dragged a small electric kettle into the bathroom, filled it, and let it run with the door closed. Steam filled the space quickly, fogging the mirror, coating everything with a wet sheen. The air felt heavy and alive.

I lay down on the tile floor, wrapped in a towel, breathing through the thick warmth. My heartbeat slowed, and the itch dulled to a pulse.

I must've drifted off.

When I woke, pale morning light was filtering through the window.

The air was cold now, the steam long gone.

For a moment, I felt hopeful.

I pulled the blanket down, expecting the smooth skin I'd had that day in Sydney.

But it wasn't healed.

It was worse.

Flakes of bloody skin clung to the sheets.

There were strands of hair too, scattered across the floor, more than I wanted to admit. I told myself it was just age, though most of them had already turned white. But all I could see was time I'd wasted—years spent studying, worrying, surviving—while life kept moving past me. Everyone else was starting families, buying their first homes, choosing schools for their children. What had I done with my life? I had the sinking feeling I was about to find out what running out of time really feels like.

Friends, families and even churchgoers had said their piece over the years. They were always spoken with that same certainty that stung more than it should have. If I were really as smart as I thought I was, they said, I wouldn't have gone into the PhD route. I would have gotten a job after my bachelor's— or even right after high school. It could had been working anything at all, even serving fries at McDonald's, just to earn a paycheck, build experience, start climbing a ladder. Anything would have been better than burying myself behind more dead weight books and doing insignificant research while the rest of the world grew up and moved on without me. Now looking at those white strands on the floor, I couldn't help but wonder if they'd been right all along.

My reflection in the mirror looked reptilian with patches of raised bumps under my jaw, tiny cuts forming at the edges of my lips. I was literally a broken mess. A diseased monster, even. I pressed a finger against my cheek. The skin gave a little, soft and hot breath, like something growing underneath. I staggered to the sink and splashed water on my face. The coolness burned. I could barely stand to look at myself.

CHAPTER 19

GNOSIS

By late morning, light pressed weakly through the thin curtains, turning the dust in the air into slow-moving flecks of gold. Through the thin walls, I could hear the sound of cereal boxes knocking against bowls, and other guests from around the world laughing and joking in their little groups in a variety of different languages, most I could recognize.

I sat at the edge of the bed, my skin tight and cracked, each movement sending a faint sting across my arms. I dabbed a small amount of topical steroid cream in slow, careful circles, leaving the cap off so I wouldn't be inefficient—the way Simeon would have wanted me to—so that it'd be easier to reach for again if I needed more later without wasting time.

The mirror showed someone paler than yesterday. Someone trying to hold myself together, layer by layer. And had obviously been failing.

I decided I wouldn't leave the hostel today, so I called the front desk to explain I was feeling extremely sick and would need the room for least an extra day. He confirmed it was okay and said he'd bill me accordingly.

My skin needed rest. My mind needed stillness.

But still, I needed distraction.

A folded newspaper, along with some crumpled receipts and a tangle of earbuds, lay on the small table in the room.

I reached for the newspaper, flipping through the pages with slow, deliberate hands. The usual noise of headlines didn't stick. Politics, weather, finance. They all felt unreal.

Then my eyes caught one small column buried near the bottom of page three of the newspaper.

Police are probing the shock death of rising opera star Marina Vale, 33, who was found dead late Monday night inside a Brooklyn bathhouse. Family members confirmed she was born on April 28, 1992, and had only just returned from a whirlwind European tour with the New York City Opera. Stunned patrons told investigators they heard a single, ear-splitting note ring through the bathhouse moments before the singer's body was discovered floating in one of the private pools. Some described the sound as so sharp it made the walls tremble. Detectives have yet to rule out foul play, despite the absence of any visible injuries. A full autopsy is now underway as police work to piece together the star's final movements and uncover what really happened in her last moments.

A young woman. Same birth year. Same month. Same day.

I squinted my eyes, scanning the article again to make sure.

She was thirty-three years old. Born on April 28th, 1992.

The exact date stamped on my birth certificate, and on every person in the murals Oakley had painted.

My lips pressed tight, heartbeat quickening.

That made… how many with the same birthdate dead now? I even took into accounts the ones I was not aware of.

Could the athlete and Oakley also have shared the same birthday?

I set the paper down, the question hovering around my head like a moth trapped in a lampshade.

But something else caught my attention. It wasn't the photo of the bathhouse or the grainy image of her body being taken away. It wasn't the missing person section. It wasn't the obituary page. It was the astrology section—a colorful ad, really—squeezed in directly below the obituaries, as if someone had strategically placed such bait there because they knew it would get the most attention.

I'd never cared for horoscopes. Not when Brendan mentioned them. Not even when the athlete at the airport brought it up. It was usually the part of the newspaper I detested and would skip with the same reflex I had for junk mail and pizza coupons.

But my eyes were drawn to the headline anyway: *Astrology Knows More About You Than You Think*.

Below it, a short blurb explained that certain Aquarius moon births fell under a rare celestial alignment tied to the eclipse later that week. It claimed those born beneath it shared not only peculiar symptoms such as 'sudden fatigue', 'vivid dreams', and a 'faint ringing in the ears', but also a 'common thread of destiny', as if the stars had drawn invisible lines between them, pulling their lives toward the same inevitable convergence.

There was a website address printed at the bottom of the column.

When I pulled out my phone, the first thing I saw was a notification from Simeon: *Jarvis, are you here for the presentation? We're waiting for you.*

Right, it was the first-year PhD talk. I stared at the message, feeling that familiar tug of obligation and guilt. But this time, it was also followed by a sudden flare of frustration. I finally understood why Vincent had told me to stop communicating with Simeon altogether. The dean's attention wasn't mentorship anymore. It was a diversion from what was more important.

I deleted the message and added Simeon to my block list.

Finally, I typed in the astrologer's website.

The website loaded slowly, as if deliberately. A black background with white text, and cheap GIF animations. A golden sigil spun at the center.

The page listed sun signs, moon signs, rising signs —just like Brendan had mentioned. There were also links related to planetary aspects, astrological houses, and compatibility charts—things I had no idea about.

Below the main content, the website featured a series of testimonials.

One person explained how studying their moon sign revealed the root of their constant clashes with their mother, and how planting roses in their garden helped channel their angry energies and repair their relationship.

Another review claimed the site's astrologer had instructed them to travel to Hawaii wearing yellow and that when they saw an omen or symbol of a scorpion, their future spouse would appear soon after.

A third testimonial described how following the astrologer's advice to sell their Toyota and buy a Porsche, based on the "vibrational power" of each brand's pronunciation had surprisingly boosted their career prospects and landed them a book deal after more than 15 years of trying to get traditionally published.

I was trying to figure out why that kind of logic made sense to them. Why would people treat the universe like a vending machine? And be convinced that planting the correct flowers or driving the right car could unlock cosmic rewards? They spoke about energies and vibrations with the same confidence a con artist uses to sell miracle water and other cure-all remedies, quoting half-remembered science as proof.

It was absurd. Laughable even. And yet, in some quiet way, I understood it. The hunger for meaning. The need for order in the chaos. The comfort for some sort of explanation from another human being. And that's why, somehow, it made sense to me too.

I also saw a simple message at the bottom of every page on the website.

Meet the astrologer in person at Williamsburg, Brooklyn for a full reading. No appointment needed.

CHAPTER 20
UNVEILING

The astrologer's office was tucked behind a weathered blue door in a narrow, brick-lined alley off Bedford Avenue in Williamsburg. It was the kind of place you'd walk past a dozen times without noticing, unless you were desperate, or curious, or because you had business to attend to.

I hesitated a while, second guessing if this was really the correct thing to do, before pushing the door open.

A small bell rang overhead as I entered. A gush of warm air wrapped around me. Inside, the air was thick with the sharp, herbal scent of burning sage. Smoke curled through the room and mingled with the musty odor of damp stone and old wooden beams that creaked faintly with my footsteps. A few stray rays of sunlight fell on potted succulents and stacks of worn books, completing the cluttered, eclectic atmosphere typical of the neighborhood.

A woman with dark hair in a ponytail and a small bindi glinting at the center of her forehead was waiting behind the counter. I wasn't sure if she'd been standing there all along or if she'd only just appeared when I looked up. On the counter in front of her was a candle teapot warmer with what looked like a freshly brewed pot of tea. Jasmine, I presumed.

All I knew was that she didn't look like the type to read crystals, cards, or speak to the dead. She also didn't look like someone that would judge. She had no flowing robes, no shimmering jewels. Just a traditional Indian sari, round glasses, and eyes that seemed to shimmer faintly like fireflies. She could had been anyone you see in the rush of New York City on a daily basis.

"Sit," she said, motioning lightly with her hand toward the chair in front of her. Her voice was calm, almost rehearsed. "I trust you've seen my ad, no doubt. I've been expecting you."

I gingerly took the seat across from her.

"I come from a family of astrologers, generation after generation, from South India," she started, her accent a mix between American and South Asian, which hinted she'd been living in this country for quite some time. "I study the stars in the traditional way, how they are truly aligned. But I've also learned the modern astrological systems used by most people in America. You can call me Rekha. Would you like some tea?"

"I'm Jarvis. And no, thank you," I said politely, as I watched her pour herself a cup.

Rekha reached for an iPad that looked recently wiped by its dried water stains, the screen gleaming under the low amber light. Its edges were studded with crystals and precious stones arranged in a perfect gradient of the chakras, which I recognized from many yoga brochures I had received over the years.

She handed the iPad over to me so I could enter my birth date, time, and location.

A digital chart bloomed on the screen, which I understood to be my birth chart. It was shaped like a wheel and divided into 12 equal sections, like pizza slices. Concentric circles nested within a larger ring, intersected by thin lines that crossed at sharp angles, forming shapes that resembled kites. It was awash in primary colors that made it look like something printed in the early '90s.

There were many strange symbols on it, which I noticed Rekha paying close attention to. Her eyes were tracing each curve and line as if trying to decipher some hidden meaning. I'd never seen them before, though I did recognize a few, like the universal symbols for male and female. Her brows were furrowed in concentration.

It was clear she recognized something in them that I could only guess at. The intensity of her focus made the symbols feel even more mysterious and charged with significance.

"Interesting, I can see you're a very unique individual indeed," she affirmed, taking a sip of tea.

"So many things have been going on with me," I replied. I wanted to tell her everything, but I stopped myself. If she listened first, her predictions would only echo what I'd said, and my scientific brain would label everything a sham. "I am unsure of who I am right now, or what I'm even supposed to do."

"I understand," she said, as she put a finger to her lips, as though for me to be quiet. "How much do you know about astrology? Are you familiar with what sun, moon, and rising signs are?

I hesitated, my mind flashing back to Brendan at the airport, asking me the same exact question so casually.

"Not really," I admitted.

She nodded understandably, as if expecting that.

"So you're born on April 28th, 1992," she started. "You'll probably be aware that you're a Taurus. Do you know why, scientifically, you're a Taurus?"

I shook my head several times.

"When you were born, the sun, when viewed from Earth, was in the constellation of Taurus," she continued, looking up at the ceiling. "Your sun sign governs your ego, your core identity, your will.

Basically, it governs the essence of who you are. You can think of it as the central fire inside you."

"My personality?" I asked. I knew just enough about astrology to sound curious, having seen my horoscope pop up on more quiz sites than I could count. "And if I'm correct, I'm stubborn and materialistic, isn't that the definition for Taurus?"

"Exactly," she said. She finished her cup, and poured another one as I noticed the wax in the candle beneath the teapot warmer had melted halfway already. "Taurus is ruled by Venus, which governs beauty, value, and what we cling to for comfort. It contains the energy of Aphrodite, the god of love. I think you will know all this. Most people know about their sun signs from newspaper columns. But not many people know about their moon and rising signs."

"Tell me more about my moon sign."

"Your moon sign reflects your emotional world and how your mind works," she explained, swaying one hand in the air. "How you feel, what moves you, what you instinctively respond to. Since the moon was in the constellation of Pisces when you were born, your emotions don't move in straight lines. They ripple like water stirred by unseen tides."

It did sound like me. But maybe it wasn't just me. Maybe there was something deeper than mere coincidence. After all, science has proven the moon moves oceans, and its gravity bends tides across continents. Who's to say the same pull couldn't reach the smaller waters of the body and stir the salt, the blood, the chemistry that keeps thought alive?

She tapped the chart on the iPad gently, at the symbol which I recognized as for Pisces.

"Pisces is co-ruled by Jupiter and Neptune," she explained. "Jupiter expands. Neptune dissolves. Together, they make empathy your native language. You don't just feel your own emotions. You absorb everyone else's, and that can sometimes be burdensome. Their moods, their memories, even echoes of things that no longer exist get attached to you. Sometimes it's a gift. Sometimes it's poison."

I rolled my eyes. "So… empathy with bad reception?"

"Something like that." Rekha smiled faintly at the joke. "You can't always tell where you end and others begin. It's beautiful, but it's dangerous if you're not grounded. You could lose yourself in the currents."

Her careful choice of words landed harder than I expected. The way she said it wasn't a metaphor anymore. It sounded like a warning.

"And the rising sign?" I pressed.

"That's the mask you wear in the world," Rekha replied. "It's how others see you when they first see you. It's your outward expression. Sometimes it can be very different from your sun or moon signs. Your rising sign is in Capricorn, so you project control, even when you're breaking apart inside. People look at you and assume you're composed, self-sufficient, reliable. You could be drowning, and they'd still hand you more weight to carry."

I noticed she had one finger pointed at the symbol for Saturn—a small circle crowned with a cross, like a sickle balanced on top of the world. She took a big sip from her tea.

"Capricorn is ruled by Saturn," the astrologer continued, clearing her throat. "Saturn contains the energy of Cronus, the old god of time, discipline, and consequence. He is the taskmaster of the heavens. In mythology, Cronus devoured his own children to keep his power. There's even a famous painting by Francisco Goya depicting it. That's the energy you radiate: restraint, endurance, sacrifice. You endure because you believe falling apart is a kind of failure. But that same gravity gives you structure."

I leaned back, biting down a scoff.

The rational part of me—the one trained to measure, to verify—was howling for evidence. Then I asked myself what proof was I actually expecting? A footnote? A peer-reviewed citation for fate?

Ever since I'd been admitted to MIT for my undergraduate studies, I'd spent years buried in data sets, not birth charts. Yet the way she spoke, the way she traced invisible forces drifting through space and pinpointed their hold on me at the moment I was born, naming the traits I'd carried ever since, felt strangely familiar. It was as though she was reading straight from my biography.

And unsettlingly so.

"That sounds like possession," I said, despite knowing that possession is more likely due to a combination of neurological and psychological phenomena, rather than supernatural. "Possessed by one of 1,728 combinations of sun, moon, and rising signs."

"Possession?" her tone sharpened, eyes glinting with quiet conviction. She tightened her grip onto the mini teacup. "You think this is about being possessed? There are actually far more than 1,728 combinations. Every planet at the time of your birth can be taken into account—the constellations where Venus, Mercury and Mars were, all the other planets, every celestial body, and even the distances between them. That includes asteroids, comets, and hypothetical objects too."

"The possibilities could be endless then," I said. "Since the universe is endless."

This astrological system seemed vast, and just as complex and intricate as any data model I had ever studied. Yet, at the same time, it was operating on a scale that made my analytical mind both nervous and intrigued.

For a moment, it almost felt like a mirror of my own work. Except in this case, the variables weren't coded in binary, plotted in graphs or transcribed with software. They were written across the heavens, scattered in vectors of light and gravity. And this was different from the way many ancient cultures linked their writing system with the heavens, such as the way Mesopotamian scribes documented every eclipse and halo around the moon.

But could the astrological system be mapped like language? Could it really guide a person's life without erasing their choice? If so, what part of me was ever mine?

"Being possessed is a force that steals your will," Rekha said, her voice snapping sharp. "But your signs and birth chart give. They guide you through life. And for now, that's all you need to know."

I slumped back, rubbing my forearm, feeling the dry cracks sting beneath my sleeve.

"What am I supposed to do now?" I asked.

"Appease Saturn," she said matter-of-factly, casually refilling her half-empty cup with more tea. "Saturn is the planet of lessons. Frankly, it's your rising sign. He governs karma, trials and timing. If you can appease Saturn, you can conquer anything. Wear stones that carry his vibration like lapis lazuli, onyx, and maybe blue sapphire if you dare. And chant his mantra—om Sham Shanaishcharaya Namah —when the night feels heavy."

Rekha began inscribing symbols onto a scrap piece of paper, murmuring words I didn't recognize. Sanskrit, I realized. I'd studied it briefly once during my undergrad, enough to recognize its roots in the Indian Vedic hymns. When she handed it to me, I saw that the symbols, when translated into English, formed the mantra I was meant to chant. Along with it, she placed a few cool and weighty tumbles of stones into my palm.

I waited, tracing my fingertips over the polished surfaces of the stones, their smoothness oddly cold against my skin. The silence between us stretched thin, broken only by the faint sound of her breath.

Then I asked quietly, "And what if none of that works?"

She smiled faintly, eyes soft. "Give it time."

I nodded slowly, unsure if it was belief or exhaustion that made me accept the answer. "How much do I owe you?"

Rekha looked at me, long and thoughtful.

She shook her head.

"No money," she said. "I prefer payment in karma."

I blinked. "What do you mean?"

"You'll know when it's time to return the favor."

The candle underneath the teapot warmer finally guttered out. The silence that followed felt thick. It was like the air itself had stopped to listen.

As I stood to leave, she added one last thing.

Her voice was calm, almost kind, "Remember, Jarvis, you have free will. Even under a planet's shadow, the choice is always yours. But the lesson will find you regardless."

CHAPTER 21

COLLISION

That night, the sky hung over the city like a bruised, heavy canvas. Shades of gray bled into black, and distant flashes of lightning pulsed faintly behind thick clouds. I couldn't shake the conversation with Rekha, the astrologer.

If all the people Oakley had painted in his murals truly shared the same birthday, then it seemed inevitable that I might be caught in the same terrible fate. And yet, Rekha's words lingered in my mind about free will, about choice. And frankly, I was still here.

Maybe I didn't have to follow that path. I didn't have to end the way I was going to. I could do everything right if I wanted to: finish the PhD, get hundreds and thousands of citations on my research, pay rent on time—and live. I could graduate, one day become a Distinguished Professor, get married, watch my kids get married, and pretend that was the point of it all.

I remembered the first time I took a helicopter over the Grand Canyon two years ago. It was during my trip to Vegas to watch the Formula 1 Las Vegas Grand Prix for a bucks party. I had gone several days and nights with almost no sleep. Too much travel, too much noise, too much of everything. But the moment the helicopter lifted off, the chaos fell away. The ground dropped beneath me until the canyon opened wide. For a strange moment, I felt calm. I watched the world shrink into something I could finally take in all at once. At that time, I had convinced myself that altitude could erase fear. That if I was high enough, nothing below could touch me. It had felt like all my limitations were just an illusion disguising how small I really was in the world.

I suddenly felt a longing to rise above the streets again. I needed to be above the alleyways and murals, to get that feeling I had when I was in that helicopter over the Grand Canyon, and see the city spread out beneath me. Maybe it wasn't just about getting air or space. Maybe it was actually about control. If I could look down on it all, I could convince myself I wasn't trapped inside it. With a calm mind, I would be able to observe it with clarity, to believe, even for a moment, that I was the one making choices and not being moved by something unseen. I had no idea of the irony, that thinking I could prove my own free will by climbing higher into the very thing that bound me.

And then, once and for all, I will be able to truly accept that no matter how tangled or senseless the mess I was in. The power to choose my next step—and to free myself—was already within me.

△△△

Faint music and laughter drifted below Hotel Hawthorne as I climbed the fire escape. When I glanced down between floors, I saw a line of sleek limousines idling by the curb with headlights glowing against the wet asphalt. Guests were stepping out in glittering evening gowns, sharp tuxedos, velvet shawls, and sequined cocktail dresses. Something was happening in the hotel, obviously. Maybe a gala, a private event, or something big enough to draw the city's wealthy and curious.

I kept climbing, one heavy step after another.

Near the top the wind hit me. It felt cold, electric, almost metallic.

New York City lights flickered below, dancing across the murals on the nearby building. From up here, they looked like ghosts trapped in pigment.

Suddenly, my phone buzzed in my pocket.

Unknown Number: *Do you want to meet?*

My first thought was Vincent. Then Oakley.

But one had gone silent. The other was dead.

I typed back quickly: *I think I'm already here.*

A pause.

Then another buzz.

Same place as last night.

Did that mean Oakley actually never died, after all?

My breath caught and I felt my hair blowing in the wind. I was at the rooftop, at the exact same place where Oakley had left me the previous night. My heart thudded against my ribs, hard enough to shake my shoulders. It felt inevitable somehow, although I didn't know why. The neon letters of *Hotel Hawthorne* buzzed above me, casting their glow across the gravel. I stood in their shadow, the light flickering over my face.

I spun around, scanning the dark corners of the roof.

"Alright, Oakley," I muttered. "If this is a joke, you win."

The wind picked up like it was whispering.

I squinted, and for a moment, I thought I saw movement near the ledge.

"Oakley?" I called out again.

Nothing.

I took a step closer, shoes scraping against the concrete.

Another shadow slid along the wall.

Then another.

And another.

It wasn't one person.

It was many.

Figures began to take shape at the edges of the roof. They were indistinct at first, like silhouettes burned into the dark. Some stood still. Some swayed as if caught in an unseen current. Their outlines shimmered. They were translucent as if made of vapor and gas.

My phone buzzed again.

You came. That means you're ready.

I swallowed, a chill crawling up my neck.

The figures were closer now. Faces began to form.

They were faces I instantly recognized.

CHAPTER 22

INITIATION

"Brendan?" I breathed.

He smiled slowly, unsettlingly, as if the motion hadn't been instructed by the muscles in his face. It was the same youthful calm. The same faint scent of hairspray that lingered in the filtered air of the airport lounge. It was him, all right. The concierge who'd brought me water, who'd stood too close, who'd said my name like he'd been waiting for me long before I arrived. Seeing him here now felt like stepping into a memory that had never ended.

Then a second figure stepped beside him wearing a metallic dress.

Jolin.

Her hair was tied back into three neat tails, each bound with metallic bands that caught the light like circuitry. Her dress had thin panels of translucent material wrapped around her arms that caught the light like sheets of glass. The shiny midnight-blue fabric was accentuated by a slit that revealed flashes of silver heels as she walked.

"What the hell are you two doing here?" I asked, my voice cracking from disbelief and exhaustion. "And you know each other?"

Brendan reached into his coat pocket. For a moment, I thought it was a weapon. A knife? A syringe? Or something small enough to hide but sharp enough to end things quietly.

My mind ran through every possibility in an instant: a recording device, a folded document with my name on it, a key, a threat disguised as a gift. But instead, he pulled out a burner phone, matte black and unmarked, the kind of thing people use when they don't want to be found.

The small phone was cheap and scuffed. He dropped it onto the concrete between us. The impact made a cracking sound, and the screen lit up one last time to the same message thread I had just read. If there was any chance to walk back from this, the chance was gone.

"You?" I whispered.

Brendan's grin widened. "You were never supposed to ignore the signs."

My pulse quickened. "What signs?"

Jolin stepped closer, her expression equally apologetic.

"We know because we were born on the same day," she said. Her voice was calm, but the words made my stomach drop. Her shoulders were tense beneath her coat, the fabric stretching slightly as she folded her arms.

"April 28, 1992," Brendan added, his tone deliberates, like a confession. "Same day. Same stars. Same storm."

Seriously? What were the chances? And how had I never realized? It made me see that Vincent calling me and Jolin 'the twins' wasn't just a metaphor.

Brendan gestured behind them with a slow sweep of his hand. I followed the motion and saw the others emerging from the shadows, standing in the shadows along the far wall. Their posture was stiff, their eyes fixed on me with a collective stillness.

There were dozens of them. They were paced out in uneven rows like silent sentinels. Some leaned against the cracked brick, half-hidden in the dark, while others stood perfectly still, their foreheads and chins faintly catching the dim red light from the exit sign.

At first, I thought they were just onlookers. Maybe squatters or wanderers from the reception happening below in the hotel. But as my eyes adjusted and their faces sharpened out of the dim, a shock tore through me as I finally realized who they were.

I recognized the man from the conference with the spiky hair stuck like it was preserved from the early 2000s. The woman I'd caught staring at me with the hearing aid. All familiar. And then there were faces from the plane, the ones who'd watched me when the turbulence hit, the man in the aisle seat who kept glancing at my hands, the woman across from me who pretended to sleep but never blinked long enough. They were all here now, scattered through the crowd, their expressions blurred by the murkiness, but unmistakable.

Their eyes didn't blink, only glistened. Their pupils looked like starving ticks, fat and glossy. Their nostrils flared in rhythm, like they were ready to inhale me. Their lips were waxy, stretched too tightly over their teeth. A cold sweat broke out on my palms, the kind that comes right before you realize you're not safe anymore. I was standing in someone else's territory, and every pair of eyes in the room had already singled me out.

Brendan lifted his chin.

"You feel it too, don't you?" he said to me. "The pull? That itch beneath your skin? You're one of us."

CHAPTER 23

ACCEPTANCE

Jolin stepped forward. Her eyes glinted in that familiar way that made me feel like she could see straight through me. It was the same look she'd given me countless times in the linguistic labs, and most recently, at the conference in Sydney.

"It's gotten worse, hasn't it?" she said sympathetically, scanning my face, neck and every part of my visible skin. "The itching, I mean."

Brendan leaned against the railing beside her, following her actions.

"It always does," he added. "Every time one of us tries to ignore it, or run from what we are, our skin gets bad again."

Jolin smiled faintly. "You've felt it. The rash. The whispers. The dreams in that language you think you invented."

"I didn't—" I said.

"You did," she cut me off, her voice smooth, and lifted both arms. "We all did. Every one of us has heard it. It started the same way. When the air hums, when the skin burns, when you think your mind is speaking through you instead of by you."

"Because we're connected," Brendan straightened, his tone sharper now. "We were all born on the same day. Same sky. Same energy. You're not crazy, Jarvis—you're Tuned."

"Tuned?" I asked, though part of me already feared the answer. "To what?"

Jolin's lips parted, reverent. "To Saraph."

The name hit me like an electric shock. It was the last thing I expected her to say. I would have expected her to mutter anything else. Maybe an insult of my falsified research, or a warning that they'd been watching me ever since the athlete and Oakley died.

But Saraph?

The name of the language I made up?

"How did you know that name?" I protested, feeling my spine jolt.

I had never mentioned that name to anyone, not even to Vincent. I had initially decided to keep the name hidden until the day I unveiled it as a climax in my research. This meant the only way they could know it was if someone had gone through my notes in secret.

The melodic twists of the word—Saraph—and the hypnotic cadences, the way it had pulled at me as if it already knew me, had already existed, and wasn't something I had invented.

The word vibrated in the air, familiar and alive.

And then I remembered something my mother once told me when I was young. She used to tell me a story about Hermes, how he once carried the first words down from Olympus in his hands and scattered them like seeds across the world, because ideas and words were gifts from gods. Some landed in poets, some in teachers, some in children who didn't yet know what to do with them.

That's when I had the revelation—the language hadn't come from me at all: it had come *to* me.

Brendan's gaze flicked up toward the skyline.

"Saraph is the name of the asteroid that came crashing onto Earth on April 28th, 1992, the day we were born," he said. "It wasn't just a celestial event. Astronomers might call it coincidence or celestial alignment, but for us, it marked a convergence. It happened in the 24 hours after the asteroid breached the solar system's outer edge, a stray body no telescope had ever logged, cutting toward Earth as if guided. That's when Saraph's energy touched Earth, and it seeded a force that would awaken in those born under that sky. It shaped our bodies, our minds, even our connection to the language."

"We—The Tuned—carry the energy of Saraph inside us." Jolin nodded. "When we're apart, we decay. Our skin burns. Our minds fray. But together, the pieces start to mend—every part of the body comes together, working in fragile harmony, as if it remembers that survival depends on unity. Each cell, each breath, each pulse aligns toward a single purpose. We were meant to remember things we never learned like phonemes, structures, and meanings. The language of the thing that lived in the stars."

"You're saying…" I started, beginning to shake uncontrollably as the revelation turned into understanding. "This Saraph, is living through us?"

"No." Brendan glanced around at the group, his eyes moving over them like he was taking attendance for something sacred. Then he smiled faintly. "Saraph is becoming through us."

"But it can't return while we're all still here," Jolin's voice softened to pity. "The energy is divided. Diluted. All of Saraph's talents and skills have been broken and divided among us."

"When one of us dies, their energy—their will, their talent that were given to us from Saraph, that have been dissolved into the population born on April 28th, 1992—flows into the rest," Brendan said. "The fewer of us there are, the stronger the connection becomes. And the last one standing…" He looked at me, eyes glinting with something like awe. "The last one becomes Saraph itself. The god reborn."

Memories flashed by, like the way I had chased that taxi in Boston with heart hammering, blanket clutched tight, moving faster than I ever thought possible—and it didn't require any work from me. It was like I had suddenly obtained a new talent. Or rather, everyone born on April 28th, 1992 had obtained a new talent.

It must have been the talent of the athlete that died being absorbed into me. And his injured leg was probably not a strained ankle or broken bone, but a rash, just like mine.

And there were more instances from my childhood that suddenly made sense. My mother had reminded me more than once that I used to be humiliatingly bad at math. I couldn't recite anything beyond the three-times table until I was almost 12. But then, during the year I started high school, something shifted. Overnight, it was as if a lock had clicked open inside my head. Algebra made sense. Trigonometry felt natural. Even early limits, derivatives, and integrals fell into place as if I'd been studying them for years. My grasp of math shot past my year level that the principal once predicted I would go into academia. My teachers called it 'talent' and 'potential,' but deep down I had always known it was something more than that.

Another example was the time I discovered the talent of spatial intuition. Back in primary school, during an Easter camp hike, I'd gotten separated from the group because I'd wandered off the trail looking for Easter eggs in a direction we weren't supposed to go. I was just a small kid straying farther than I realized. There were no phones back then, and even if there had been, there would've been no signal that deep in the bush. But instead of panicking, I walked with a steady certainty, as if something in me already knew the way. Not long after, I stepped back onto the main track, right in front of the teachers before they had even fanned out to search for me. I never spoke about it to anyone. I thought I was just young. But now I realized a contestant on a survival game show who was born on the exact same day as me was attacked by a snake during filming and hadn't made it. The thought landed with a cold, unwelcome clarity.

As much as I wanted to deny it, a quiet certainty pressed in from somewhere deep within me. My shoulders tensed, my breath thinned, and my fingers curled unconsciously toward my palms. No matter how hard I fought it, I knew, with a heaviness that settled in my chest, that I was indeed, one of them.

CHAPTER 24

FACEOFF

The air between us thinned. It felt sharp and cold. I stepped back, the smell of disinfectant and ozone from the rooftop vents stinging my nose.

"So it was true, you two tried to kill me," I said, my voice shaking but sharp. "Brendan, you mixed something into the water. And Jolin gave me that poisoned chocolate."

"But you survived," she said with purpose. "That means Saraph favored you. You were the only one that had the gift of reviving this lost language. You also stayed true to the command of being a Tuned. You destroyed the others—The Strays—born on the same date as us that never realized who they were, ensuring that only the few who chose to form this

Merge could live on. You carry one of his most prized talents."

Brendan tilted his head. His eyes were distant, almost reverent. "You should be grateful, Jarvis." He took a slow step forward. "The Strays and the Earthborn die. The rest—us from the heavens— remain."

Around us, the others began murmuring in that strange, melodic language of Saraph that I thought I invented.

"Because of you last night, the Saraph language is now alive after you taught it to us," Jolin said. "It may seem insignificant to you, but it's a major step in Saraph's reincarnation into this world because we can now have direction conversations with Him. And to be honest… I've always known that, considering I've always been the linguist working by your side."

"To have direct conversation with a fake deity?" I protested. "You're talking about a language I made up at two in the morning. You're treating it like scripture."

It took me a while to realize there was a rhythm beneath the murmurs around me.

They were singing.

The melody rolled off their tongues like a hymn, swelling with the grandeur of an opera, obviously obtained from the opera singer that had recently died in the bathhouse. Each note trembled through the air, echoing off the concrete walls. The sound was layered, haunting, almost reverent, as if the city itself were holding its breath to listen.

And yet, as I listened, a thought began to claw its way through me. *Had I really taught them?* Had something happened while I wasn't there—while I slept, or blacked out, or simply forgot—forcing me to do something I never meant to as though I was… possessed by Saraph?

The gaps in my memory pulsed like open wounds. I tried to remember the night before, the words I might have spoken, but the harder I searched, the less I trusted that any of it had been mine to give.

Brendan spread his arms.

"Every one of us here in The Merge was born under Saraph's shadow and have chosen to be Tuned," he said. "We all carry His essence. It may be divided, scattered, incomplete but the death of one strengthens the rest. We all want the same thing, to be the final vessel, Jarvis. To be the true reincarnation of Saraph."

A shiver slid down my spine.

The idea wasn't just religious.

It was competitive.

Savage.

They weren't a congregation. They were predators in waiting, praying for each other's downfall under the guise of faith. Anyone could see this. Why couldn't they? I thought of what would happen when only a couple of us were left. I could picture the circle tightening, knives sharpening, hands clasped in ritual for the last throne, to inherit whatever power we were all being shaped for.

"Who started this whole congregation?" I demanded clenching my fists. "Who recruited and brainwashed you to do all this?"

The murmuring stopped. The crowd in The Merge shifted. Their heads lowered and their shoulders dipped. Those at the front stepped back to create a narrow path.

From behind them, a man stepped forward through the newly made path. He was tall and composed. His posture was quiet and had authority given to him, the weight of decades I knew he hadn't lived. The immaculate black cardigan he wore seemed to swallow the light, and his presence pressed against my chest like gravity itself, as if he carried the patience and knowing of a lifetime in every measured step.

"I did," he said, his voice smooth as smoke. "And now you're home."

"Vincent?" I said, looking at my PhD advisor's familiar face.

CHAPTER 25
ORDINATION

Vincent's eyes were calm and absolute as they swept over me, like he was weighing the worth of my very soul. For a moment, I couldn't move. This wasn't some stranger or random fanatic you'd find preaching to ducklings in the Boston Common after a drunken night out.

This was *Vincent*.

My doctoral advisor.

The man who'd written my recommendation letters, who'd sat beside me through endless seminars, who'd once told me that research was about data and results, not reputation.

My heart lurched. "Vincent… what are you doing?" My voice cracked as I took a step back. "How could you? You're a scientist. An academic.

You're supposed to believe in data, not… whatever this is. You know this whole cult thing is all in the mind."

He didn't flinch. "I still believe in data," he said softly. "But you never understood what it really measures."

I stared at him, waiting for the joke, the flicker of irony, the self-aware smirk he used when challenging my theories in the lab. But there was nothing. Only that steady, unblinking calm. I wasn't entirely sure what I was hoping to accomplish by holding his gaze.

"You're talking about killing people," I said finally, the words tasting like ash. "Like me. Like everyone else who shares our birthday? That's like—I don't know—the lives of 300,000 people. You're talking about—"

"Fulfilment," Vincent said quietly. "Awakening. Surgical correction."

I suddenly grasped how wide that net stretched. Like how many people shared my exact birth date, and to an extent, under the same sun, moon, and even rising, signs that I would need to kill. The thought of this cruelty being justified as right made my stomach twist.

"There are still too many like you, like me, tied to the same cosmic pattern diluting the energy," Vincent replied, looking away over the New York skyline.

"This why you must act in accordance to the divine map—or watch it slip away."

"So your grand plan is to either recruit or eliminate the three hundred thousand people who share our birthdate—worldwide?" I asked, feeling the ridiculousness of my own words.

Vincent inclined his head, as if my horror were something he'd already accounted for. Maybe he had. Maybe he'd been waiting for this exact moment—for me to realize what I'd done, or what he'd made me do. And he wanted to make sure I wasn't sidetracked, hence the reason to tell me to cut all contact with Simeon.

Or maybe it wasn't guilt he'd anticipated, but obedience, the kind that comes after panic wears off and you start to believe there's no way out so you agree to every bargain.

His words hung in the air like a static charge, and it felt like I was waiting for lightning to strike.

I searched his face, desperate for some flicker of reason. Something human. But his expression was as steady as ever. It was the same expression I'd seen in weekly meetings, when we walked past in the Infinite Corridor, and even when he'd corrected my syntax charts or debated field data over coffee.

I shook my head.

"That's mythology, Vincent," I said. "That's not science. How long have you been orchestrating this cult?"

He tilted his head, considering. "Longer than you. Long enough to see the patterns form. Long enough to understand why I chose you. Every discovery has a cost. You should know that better than anyone."

In that moment, I realized something worse than betrayal.

He wasn't insane. He wasn't doing this for money or fame. He wasn't doing it because he wanted to see how far I'd follow.

He did it because he believed every word he was saying like it was actually the truth and nothing but the truth.

Vincent's gaze fixed on me, steady and unyielding.

"I'll give you a choice," he said slowly. "You can join The Merge as a Tuned, or you can be another Stray living among the Earthborn."

I let out a nervous laugh. "Join The Merge and make it my purpose to kill everyone born on our same birthdate? Are you insane?"

Vincent stepped closer, the city lights glinting faintly off his shoulders.

"There's only one thing you need to do," Vincent's words were cold and ceremonial, as if I were being inducted into a nightmare. "All you need to do from now on is to follow the seven tenets."

I felt my stomach drop.

"Seven tenets?" I echoed.

"The Seven Tenets of Saraph," Vincent clarified, his voice almost tender. "You've already lived some of them without knowing."

I felt my throat tighten.

From his pocket, he pulled out a piece of fibrous paper and let it go, watching it drift through the wind as though he had the patience—or the arrogance—to believe he commanded the elements themselves.

The sheet spiraled upward, catching the red glow of the neon before landing in my hand, like it had obeyed him willingly.

The Seven Tenets of Saraph

1. Dress not your age — so that no Stray or Earthborn may ever guess your birthday. Time is the first illusion.

2. Support those within The Merge as they are yourself — for separation is the grandest deception. Unity is the only truth.

3. Reveal not your identity — not to spouse, parent, or friend. The uninitiated will always seek to destroy what they cannot comprehend.

4. Question not the divinity of Saraph — for thought itself can rot purity.

5. Seek salvation only through The Merge — for salvation is alignment, not freedom.

6. Know that punishment for transgression is death, and the sacrifice of talents — that all gifts may return to Saraph.

7. Accept that Saraph is greater than the Earthborn of this world — for the Earth and all who dwell upon it have failed their own design.

After reading the small pamphlet etched with faint gold lines, part of me wanted to laugh. Yet the words hung in the air like hooks, and I could feel them finding purchase in places I didn't know were still raw.

Vincent smiled faintly.

"Once you accept these seven tenets, you officially become part of The Merge, and you will never have to struggle alone, Jarvis," he said. "You were meant to be awakened. Your PhD? Secure. Your tenure? Guaranteed. Your research? Uninterrupted. You don't need to worry about Simeon or anyone anymore. I will make sure you get enough contracts to never worry about money. Your skin rashes won't hold you back anymore. You'll be able to sleep without scratching, eat anything you want, attend any social event. You will have a life and a story to be told for generations."

The offer was impossible, obscene, and seductive all at once. It promised power, safety, immortality of name and spirit—but at the cost of innocence, morality, and life itself.

Brendan and Jolin moved closer, circling me like predators, their eyes catching the faint starlight.

Around us, the group was singing louder. The notes came out as a low, resonant vibration that grew into a single operatic note. Then words. The language of Saraph. The one from my dreams. The one I'd seen whispered through Oakley's murals.

"Join The Merge," they sang in Saraph. "Hail Saraph!"

They sang in unison now as if it was by the same mind, the chant swelling into something both holy and sickening, the rhythm clawing into my chest.

"Join The Merge just as you were about to two nights ago with Oakley, before you ran away from Saraph's attunement," Jolin said, her voice threading through the music like smoke. "Show your allegiance, and you'll see your old self was never real. You *are*, and have always been, one of us. You just haven't admitted it yet."

I shook my head, panic and fury colliding. "I—No! I won't!"

"I was once like you too," Jolin added gently. "I was skeptical, brittle, full of excuses about research and personal space. I was broke. Did I ever tell you I was adopted and abandoned? I thought I could be in control. I thought my insomnia, the tremors, the burning skin, the way food turned to acid in my mouth—all of it—were just symptoms of stress. But they weren't. They were signs of resistance, until I joined The Merge."

"Do you remember the way I was watching out for you in the business lounge?" Brendan cut in, his tone sharp but trembling beneath the surface. "Every little thing I did, from getting you free entry, getting a private room for you to make sure you would be healthy. I did them for you because I knew one day you would join The Merge too."

"Listen to me, Jarvis," Jolin pleaded again. "Ever since I joined The Merge, every single one of my papers has been accepted on the first submission. No revisions. No rejections. Reviewers practically call my work visionary."

She stepped closer, eyes gleaming with a confidence I'd never once seen in her back at MIT. As I watched the intensity in her eyes, I couldn't tell whether the radiance in them was real or manufactured by whatever she'd given herself over to.

"I bought my own place in Back Bay—where the millionaires in Boston reside," she continued. "I have no mortgage or debt on my brownstone loft. And my health, Jarvis… my body feels invincible. I used to bruise if someone bumped into me in the hallway. But now? Not even a scratch holds for more than a minute. I haven't been sick in years—not even a cold. And there's one thing I've been keeping a secret. I'm recently engaged."

I turned to look at Vincent. His smile didn't fade. It was as though Jolin's words had amplified his expression. It stayed perfectly in place with patience, serenity, and almost saintly. It was the kind of smile that promised salvation.

"Just remember our fates are bound," he finally said, his head tilting with a calm so controlled it made the hairs on the back of my neck rise. "The astrology, the birth date, the alignment of stars—they all tie us together. Every move you make, every breath you take… we know who you are, how you are feeling, and the type of interactions you will come across. Every reflection, every face you meet, every moment of your life will be marked in the pattern Saraph watches. And one day, your face will join the murals down there. I will personally paint your mural, if it comes to that."

My nerves snapped tight like wires, staring over the edge of the rooftop. There were already people down there—probably other Tuned from The Merge—that had taken over Oakley's job and were in the middle of painting other faces.

The murals looked like a congregation of the damned. The faces were marked with pinhole pupils and frozen smiles that seemed to scream beneath the paint. They were all caught in some endless struggle. Each person was vying against the other, clawing for space, for air, for survival. Some were well aware they were part of The Tuned, but decided to be part of The Strays. Others were blankly innocent, unaware they had already been trapped in that same cursed fate.

And there, on the nearest wall, I saw Oakley's face, freshly painted. For a moment, it felt like he was looking back at me, alive again in someone else's design.

I could almost feel the pulse of that asteroid's energy pressing against me.

Jolin's voice came closer, silk over steel.

"The cosmos is patient," she said. "Fate is patient. Saraph is patient. And we're all in it."

My knees weakened.

The city stretched beneath me, endless and indifferent.

The wind bit at my skin, whipped through my hair, and my heart thudded so hard it hurt. I could *feel* the pull of them—the gravity of the cult, the bulk of everyone born on my date—alive and waiting.

And all I had to do was give in, and I could be freed from all this, at least for a little while.

"Decide now," Vincent commanded, his voice cutting through the chant. "Live and wield the power, or deny it and become one more face among the dead, preserved in paint for eternity."

I backed away until the railing pressed into my palms.

My breaths came shallow and fast. The chant rose around me, echoing through steel and concrete, through blood and bone.

My heartbeat matched its rhythm.

I could *see* it now. The inevitability. Every star, every planet, every alignment. They were all watching. It was truly like being possessed.

The chant grew louder, the group swaying in unison, their eyes bright with hunger and awe.

My pulse raced, my body trembling.

Murder.

Destiny.

Survival.

In my head, I recited the mantra Rekha had instructed me to: om Sham Shanaishcharaya Namah.

The choice pressed down like a storm.

But even through the terror, a spark of defiance flared inside me.

No.

I clutched the tumbles of lapis lazuli and onyx in my pocket, their smooth edges pressing cool against my sweaty palm.

I wouldn't let them. Neither fate, nor Saraph, nor any planet, god or demon would decide who I was because I had free will.

I turned toward the fire escape and broke into a run.

No one moved to stop me. Not Vincent, not Jolin, not Brendan. Not any of The Tuned. They only watched, silent and expectant, as I slipped past the edge of their shadowed congregation and down the narrow staircase.

I was finished being the one observed. It was my turn to watch back. For the first time, I knew exactly where I needed to go next.

CHAPTER 26

DISCERNMENT

Even though it was nearing 2 a.m., I hurried onto the L train bound for Williamsburg, making my way to Rekha's office. The hour felt wrong and unnatural for a visit like this. But then again, this was New York City where time rarely mattered. And she was probably already used to it.

I dashed through the familiar lanes and knocked a few times, only to find the front door locked. The lights inside, however, were still on. I wondered if I should call her and tell her I was outside. As I circled around the building, I found the back door slightly ajar, hanging open just enough to feel as if it had been left that way for me alone. So, I slipped inside through the rear entrance without thinking, stepping into the quiet, dimly lit practice as if I'd been expected all along.

The air was thick with the same incense, as though time had stopped since the last time I was here. Smoke curled lazily around shelves of stones, crystals, and celestial charts like last time. Through the tall, dust-specked window, an amber haze hung over the cables of the Brooklyn Bridge, casting the city in a muted, otherworldly glow.

My hands trembled slightly as I discovered Rekha standing by the counter, like the first time I saw her. She was still, silent, and composed in that way she had, like she'd been waiting there long before I arrived. In her hand was a mug, and by the smell of it, coffee.

I stepped beside the wooden chair across from her, one leg brushing against it as I readied myself to sit. The chair creaked against the tiled floor. The scent of incense coiled around me, thick and fragrant, blurring the edges of the dim light that filtered through the curtains.

"Why didn't you tell me there was an asteroid the day I was born?" I asked, my voice unsteady, angry. "The people I met, they said I'm tied to it. They call it Saraph. They say it's fate, destiny. But I feel trapped, like every choice I make has already been written. I need you to tell me everything. What god or demon this asteroid has the energy of, and how I can break free from it."

Rekha's eyes softened and she covered her mouth to yawn. Her expression became heavy with something between pity and resignation as she held onto her iPad that displayed my birth chart, and then took a sip of coffee.

She gestured toward the charts and maps of constellations pinned behind her, their thin paper edges fluttering slightly from the draft of a nearby fan.

"Destiny is a framework, Jarvis—a lattice of tendencies, influences, and possibilities," she said quietly, like it was a secret. "I did not tell you before because I didn't want to corrupt your path with fear. I wanted you to carry hope. Free will is what bridges the stars and your life. Without it, everything collapses into fatalism."

"But Saraph—the asteroid—it feels alive," I exhaled slowly, struggling to process her words. Tears were forming in my eyes. "It's like it's pulling everyone around me into the same orbit. Why didn't you warn me?"

Rekha nodded gravely, and stood up to walk around her practice.

"Saraph was once thought to be a celestial being, a sibling of the ancient artisan god Tvashtr in Vedic lore," she said. "Legends say it tried to create its own world, to separate from the heavens. Its ambition was so great it was cast out, becoming a wandering asteroid. It's not demonic, nor is it a god. It doesn't destroy. Instead, it amplifies what's already within you, revealing both fractures and potential."

"So what does this mean?" I asked, both my hands on the desk.

She leaned forward slightly, her bracelets clinking.

"Look closely, Jarvis," she said, pointing at the iPad before her, at the circle where 9 o'clock would be. Her breath lingered with a warm trace of coffee. "Saraph is right there on your horizon, rising in conjunction with you. It is aligned with your life, woven into your very being. It reflects the struggles, the tensions, the choices you face. Those are not punishments. They are tools. Saraph isn't here to destroy you. It is you, showing what happens when you try to run from what's already inside your heart."

Saraph wasn't a distant threat or a death sentence. It was a mirror, a challenge, a living part of me demanding awareness, forcing me to navigate the tension between fate and choice.

And somehow, that made the world feel both larger and more within reach than it had moments before.

I frowned. "So I should fight? Or should I accept?"

"You cultivate mindfulness, Jarvis," she said, moving her head that I was unable to tell if she was shaking or nodding. "Charity, meditation, breath work. Prayer beads, and mantras are practices to balance the energies you cannot fully control.

Regarding the asteroid's presence, there is no guaranteed action you can take to control it. You can only harmonize with it, observe, and live consciously."

"So there's no way to prevent Saraph's plan?" I leaned back, trying to absorb it all. "I might as well die."

"There is no plan that dictates your actions," she said firmly, walking around again her shop gain, tidying the windchimes hanging from the ceiling. "Only tendencies, energies, currents. You must move like a gardener, planting thorns in some places, nurturing growth in others. The asteroid—along with all the asteroids like Vesta, Juno and Pallas—is like a wind. You cannot stop it, but you can choose how to stand in it. You must learn to bend, and how to shield yourself."

I looked down at my hands. The tension in my fingers eased slightly, though my skin still itched from the stress of the night before.

"And the others?" I asked. "The ones in the cult… Vincent, Jolin, Brendan… what about them?"

"They follow what they believe is destiny," the Indian astrologer said, as she reached into a glass cabinet crowded with brass Ganeshas, jade Buddhas, and faded marigold garlands that had long since turned brittle. "You follow what you know. Do not mistake their path for yours. They are caught in patterns that resonate with their birth energies, just as you are with yours. But you are not bound to their choices. Only you can decide what you allow into your life."

I felt a flicker of hope. It was fragile but it was real. Free will.

The power to act, to refuse, to survive on my terms.

Rekha came back over and handed me a small set of prayer beads, smooth and cool in my palm.

"Use these if you wish," she said, finishing her coffee and sliding the cup away from her. "They are tools, not solutions. Meditation, breath, charity, and awareness of your own actions are the real defenses," she said, her eyes steady. "Your Mars in Pisces reminds you that thorns must exist to allow flowers to bloom. Your Venus in Aries reminds you that passion must be tempered with patience."

I nodded slowly, the weight in my chest lifting just a fraction.

There were forces I could not fully understand, and people I could not control. But I could control myself.

I could act deliberately, resist, observe.

As I left the astrologer's office and walked away, the sight of the Williamsburg Bridge unfolded like a spine across the morning sky. The Wythe Hotel glowing faintly to my right, and the scent of fresh bread drifted from a late-night bakery on Bedford. The wind against my face and the first warm smear of sunrise made me feel for a brief movement that my choices were still mine.

For the first time in what felt like months, I allowed myself to breathe without panic.

Free will, I realized, was not a single act.

It was continuous, moment by moment.

And if I could navigate it, perhaps I could survive the chaos of Saraph, the cult, and the cosmic designs that seemed bent on consuming me.

CHAPTER 27
ORDAINED

The next time I saw Vincent at MIT, it was on Monday. He didn't mention Saraph, The Seven Tenets, or Hotel Hawthorne. He didn't mention how he met Brendan, or why the rooftop was their designated meeting place. It was as if everything about The Merge had simply slipped from his mind.

He greeted me in the corridor outside the linguistics lab with the same easy smile and professional calmness he used when chatting with visiting faculty. His Rolex watch caught the light as he adjusted his gold cuff, then came the faint scent of expensive cologne hanging in the air. His shoes barely made a sound against the polished floor. For a moment, I almost wondered if I'd imagined everything.

He laughed at something trivial and carried himself like a man who'd never spoken about cosmic patterns or divine energy. He was an academic discussing grant proposals and organizing conferences, not a prophet planning annihilation.

During our weekly meeting, he only mentioned that the contract for my new teaching position had been updated and that I would receive the email soon. He added that the pay rate would be at the doctorate level, even though I hadn't officially graduated yet. He asked if I needed any help with my proposal for the upcoming candidacy presentation. I told him I was fine. He nodded, looked deep into my eyes and assured me I would be able to pass it.

△△△

I walked back to my office with my mind still wrapped around the astrologer's words. Even amidst everything I'd discovered on the rooftop of Hotel Hawthorne, life continued in its mundane rhythm.

On the way, I passed Simeon in the Infinite Corridor. He was pinning up a poster on the notice board, announcing that the department was seeking a new PhD candidate for a project on the acquisition of an endangered language. It was complete with deadlines and scholarship information. As he heard my footsteps, he glanced sideways, as if checking whether I'd noticed. But I didn't give him the satisfaction. I kept walking, treating him the same way I treated the occasional campus visitor who wandered into the wrong hallway. He was present, but totally irrelevant to me.

As I sat in my office, preparing to delve back into my PhD research, the door to my office burst open.

A woman suddenly rushed in, clutching a stack of notebooks and folders. Her sneakers squeaked against the polished floor like she had sprinted the length of the Infinite Corridor after getting lost in it. She was humming a low, clear line from the famous opera, *The Magic Flute*.

"Oh, hi there, I'm Sophia," she said breathlessly, cheeks flushed. Her foundation looked slightly uneven in the light, but the rest of her makeup was flawless. "I—uh—I just ran all the way from Back Bay. No one told me that the trains and buses were on strike, and the taxi was way overpriced. So I decided do it by foot. I didn't know I could move this fast."

I stood up halfway, unsure whether to offer her a seat or just let her catch her breath.

"You must be Jarvis, right?" she added between gasps, setting her notebooks down on my table. I noticed the cover was decorated with beautiful artworks of exotic animals and majestic plants in stunning poses. I had no doubt she'd drawn them herself. She straightened her loose cardigan and smoothed the creases in her tucked-in blouse. "I'm a visiting researcher from Western Sydney University. I'm doing a post-doc in Psychopharmacology. Just started this year, actually. Are you aware of Professor Caroline Stone? She told me a lot of great things about you. She said you'd be the best person to collaborate with on my research. I study drugs for stuttering. I heard you know phonetics. I think we could actually make some progress."

I noticed the subtle signs. The way she sang effortlessly, sustaining the notes of the opera line even after running all the way from Back Bay. The calm rise and fall of her breath that defied the distance she'd just covered. Her face seemed slightly inflamed, flushed beneath the sheen of makeup, and there was a faint dryness around her ears.

"Oh?" I said, stepping closer as she picked up a notebook. "Do you have a researcher's profile or something I can look at?"

"I've already emailed you," she said, her voice quick and eager, almost desperate to prove she belonged. "It should be in your inbox. Just search my name."

I opened my laptop, typing as she spoke. Her message appeared at the top of my inbox, sent barely an hour ago. Attached was a link to her university research profile. I clicked.

Her photo appeared beside a clean, institutional layout. It was the kind I'd seen a thousand times before. It included full name and title, pronouns, university crest, academic bio and an array of contact information. Underneath, the usual details were arranged with clinical precision.

Department: School of Science

PhD Thesis: Psychopharmacological Interventions and the Neurolinguistics of Stuttering: A Study on Speech Disruption and Cognitive Dissonance

Date of Birth: April 28, 1992

I turned back to look at her. She looked older, or younger. I couldn't decide which. But it was the exact birthdate I'd been searching for, like seeing your own lottery numbers appear on a stranger's ticket. The coincidence hit with a quiet, electric dread, and for a moment, reality felt thin, like I'd stepped into a version of the world that wasn't entirely mine.

"Where were you born, by the way?" I asked her, faking a curious smile.

"Melbourne," she replied, cautiously.

"And the time?" I asked, lifting my gaze to her in a slow and deliberate motion to study her face as if she was something fragile and fascinating that I wasn't sure I was allowed to touch.

"I think around 1 p.m." She frowned. "On April 28, 1992. Why?"

"That's the same age as me!" My pulse thundered. I hoped it didn't look too forced. "Taurus sun and Pisces moon?"

"Astrology?" she froze, utterly confused. "All I know is that I'm a Taurus."

"Don't worry," I replied with a laugh.

Another person born on the same day.

Another potential target in this twisted cosmic hierarchy.

The old surge of panic and temptation rose. It was the same impulse Vincent and The Merge had fed me for months, maybe years. The thought of absorbing her knowledge, skills and brilliance was beyond human lust and greed. All I had to do was offer her kindness, get her to trust me, and eventually, want to repay me.

"Tell me," I said, forcing my voice to stay steady, and gestured to a chair next to her to sit down. "What exactly do you do at Western Sydney University?"

She grinned, brushing a loose strand of hair behind her ear.

"I design and test compounds aimed at easing stuttering, everything from oral medications to injectable agents," she spoke like it was lyrics of a song. "We run pharmacokinetic studies, trial dosing, and behavioral assays. Mostly lab work, a lot of careful measuring, and then watching how small changes ripple through speech patterns."

"You inject people?" I asked, surprised by how clinical the question sounded.

"Sometimes," she said lightly, as if announcing a weekend plan. "They're cleaner for certain mechanisms. That's for sure. But don't picture me as a mad-scientist doing theatrics works. No, please don't. What I do are protocols, approved by ethics, and a mountain of paperwork. I like it because it's tactile. It's kind of like mixing compounds and seeing how molecules behave. Call it a ridiculous sort of talent that I've been interested since I was young, after watching the TV show, *Animorphs*."

She laughed, a bright, easy sound that dissolved some of the room's tension.

"And yes," she continued, all serious again, despite the smile never leaving her face. "It's very thrilling when a trial shows even a small improvement in stuttering. Better than coffee, despite being told I shouldn't drink too much of that."

I nodded back as friendly as I could. Her casualness and the way she spoke of delicate syringes and controlled trials as if they were crafts, deepened the ache inside me. Her profession had a pull that was like a quiet urge, to take and possess that competence. I wondered what I could do with her talent. What sort of sublime venom would I be able to create? What sort of corrosive effect it could produce, and how it might alter thoughts and actions to my advantage.

Yet watching her, so light and human, made the impulse feel obscene. The talent that brought her joy, even as her skin tortured her with pain, was something I had no right to possess. When she spoke about her published journals and book, something bright flickered through her as if she became a different person entirely.

The work belonged to her. It had been carved by years of study and a peculiar, private genius. And yet, as the thought of a familiar itch running across my arms and the memory of past horrors flashed in my mind, I forced myself to pause.

I breathed deeply, recalling the astrologer's words: free will.

But the concept wouldn't repeat in my mind.

Was that because I didn't have it? Or had I already spent it somewhere along the way and traded it for comfort, recognition, and the illusion of control? Maybe that was the cruelest part of destiny. Not the certainty of what was coming, but the quiet conviction that I'd chosen it. I wondered if free will wasn't freedom at all, but a story we told ourselves to make obedience bearable.

Sophia was extraordinary. Not just because of her life choices or her expertise in chemistry, but because of how she approached her explanation. Her formulas sounded like everyday speech, experimental data transformed into patterns, and somehow, she could translate complex pharmacology into rhythms that resonated with anyone who listened.

I remembered my mother reading stories to me. It was the comfort in her voice, the safety in narrative, the quiet magic of someone creating worlds with words. She once told me the tale of Paracelsus, the wandering alchemist who tried to distil the essence of life itself. According to her, he believed every element hid a secret soul, waiting to be transformed by the right hands. I used to think it was just a story about potions and miracles, but now it felt like something else, that a reminder that even creation can demand sacrifice. That warmth, that artistry, stirred something protective in me rather than destructive.

I moved toward her carefully and reached for a bottle of champagne sitting on my desk. "By the way, would you like a drink?" I asked. "It's Armand de Brignac."

"Water is fine," she said with a polite smile.

"Lemon?"

"Just plain water."

I crouched slightly as I opened the cabinet beside my desk. The glass was conveniently waiting there, right next to the bottle of spring water, and the packets of vegan chocolate, the same kind Jolin had brought me.

I took out the glass and set it down with quiet precision. I poured the water slowly, the liquid catching the lamplight in trembling ripples. Then I lifted the glass and gave it a gentle swirl, my eyes never leaving hers.

"There you go," I said, offering her the glass of water. "Just water. For you."

She looked up, confused but thankful.

My pulse slowed as I watched her drink, realizing that the act of giving, rather than taking, carried a different kind of power.

It was a power that didn't cost someone else's life.

"You sure you don't want some alcohol?" I asked again. "It's really fine champagne from France."

"I'd love to, but unfortunately I can't," she said, holding the half-empty cup in her hand. "I have eczema, and alcohol makes it worse."

"Really?" I nodded, keeping my tone calm, precise, attentive. "Where?"

Without hesitation, she rolled up her sleeve and revealed the rash along her forearm. The red cracks looked almost luminous under the overhead light. She did it with a hint of annoyance, the practiced motion of someone who'd shown it countless times before.

Instinctively, I reached out and placed my hand over it. Her skin was warm, trembling slightly under my touch.

For a moment, the air between us felt charged, droning with a low static.

Then I pulled my hand away, revealing healthy skin.

"What eczema?" I asked her. "Your skin was already perfect when you arrived."

It wasn't illusion or coincidence. We were both really under the current of Saraph, and when our bodies connected, the sickness dissolved as if it had never existed. It felt like a sign, the living proof that Saraph's energy renewed itself whenever two people of the same date came together.

She opened her mouth to argue, but no sound came out.

I chuckled lightly and began typing an email to Vincent that I had found another Stray, and that she was right in the room with me. *Should I turn her into a Tuned and invite her to join The Merge? Or should I expedite the rebirth of Saraph?*

"Even I have sensitive skin sometimes," I said, keeping my tone light as my hands drifted over the keyboard, each keystroke masked beneath the sound of my own voice so she wouldn't notice what I was doing. "Our bodies don't always behave the way we expect, and sometimes we heal without even realizing it."

I turned back to my laptop screen and hovered the mouse over the send button, unsure whether I should send the email to Vincent.

And in that moment, I understood something crucial. Knowledge and talent were not mine to steal. Stories, experiences, and discoveries were to honor, witness, and nurture.

The more I allowed myself to feel that, the more my mind felt centered.

It was a lesson, like a thorn turned into a flower. I could exist in the same world as The Tuned and The Strays, born on the same day, without surrendering to the darkness Vincent and The Merge had imposed. I could choose my actions. I could protect. I could guide. Or I could kill.

And for now, I let the mini war in my mind play out like a game of cat and mouse.

CHAPTER 28

HABIT

Back in my Beacon Hill apartment that night, the hum of the fluorescent lights was oddly soothing. Through the window, I could see the faint glow of the State House dome a block away, and the rhythmic flash of ambulance lights washing over the nearby buildings in blue and red.

Outside, the tour guide lingered at the final stop—my building, once one of Boston's oldest hotels opened in 1899, before it was carved into apartments. His voice rose and fell beneath the streetlights, carrying stories of the city's ghostly past.

For the first time in weeks, I had finally paid my bills. The weight of overdue notices and automated warnings had lifted, at least for now. I even treated myself to something small—a late dinner from

Quincy Market. Fried clams, a lobster roll slick with butter, and a cup of New England clam chowder that steamed against the cold air. It was the kind of food I hadn't tasted in over 30 years—before I was formally diagnosed with my allergies—something I used to walk past and think, someday, when my allergies go away. Now, after one strange, stolen night, they had. When the check came, I left a 40% tip and drew a small smiley face on the receipt—a quiet way of saying thanks, or maybe just proof that for once, I was finally like one of everyone else.

After finishing a glass of wine, my skin looked healthier in the bathroom mirror, almost vibrant under the harsh light. I couldn't help but stand there a few extra minutes admiring myself before brushing my teeth. The rash and irritation that had been creeping along my jawline were gone. No itching, no redness, no allergic flare-ups from the seafood, egg, or gluten—nothing. It was as if my body had decided to forgive me for all the stress, the skipped meals, the weeks of living off water and panic.

Looking back, I couldn't explain why I hesitated when Vincent revealed The Seven Tenets of Saraph. As evident now, my body had repaired itself. My skin no longer cracked under stress, the tremors have stilled, and sleep comes without melatonin or any medical intervention. The noise in my head has quieted to a perfect hum like a musical. Money moves toward me as if it remembers my name. My work is funded, my future secured, my mind stripped clean of doubt. It was as if my obedience had been recognized and I'd been rewarded.

Papers lay scattered across my desk. Half-filled notebooks were stacked like small towers. Reference books were splayed open to pages of syntax trees and phonological charts. Several voice recorders and portable drives were tangled among the mess, their indicator lights blinking faintly like small, restless thoughts waiting to be replayed.

My laptop sat open to the washed glow of my inbox. At the top was a university-wide bulletin from the Provost that only appeared when something had gone terribly wrong. It read that a visiting researcher from Australia had been found dead a few hours earlier on the wet stone steps outside the MIT Chapel. There were no signs of life when campus police arrived. From the scratches and wounds covering her skin, the incident was being treated as an intentional act of self-harm.

I deleted the email. The apartment was quiet except for the soft tap of my keyboard and the editing of my document that would decide my admission to candidacy—due in just a few days.

Then my phone buzzed, slicing through the stillness.

A single text appeared. It had no sender name, only the message.

I immediately pulled up the list from my binder I'd been building. It contained names, photos, coordinates of people born on April 28, 1992. Each entry was a pin on a map that seemed to stretch farther every night: a student in Kyoto, a journalist in Toronto, an accountant in Berlin. I'd found them through university archives, leaked census files, social media posts—and of course, underground networks of other Tuned, silently supporting each other in secret. The list wasn't complete, obviously, but it was enough to move on. Discipline looks a lot like obsession when you're dedicated enough.

Alongside it, I kept a second list of upcoming events and conferences near those areas, cross-referenced with others who had already pledged their souls to The Merge. I had budgeted and brainstormed how I could make their gatherings and events successful so they could convert more Strays to Tuned. I had promoted them through my own newsletters, slipped their names into grant proposals, and aligned them with highly relevant sponsors who had no idea what they were truly funding.

My fingers hovered above the keyboard, then moved.

I thumbed a reply without thinking too much about tone or implication: *On my way.*

I hit send.

The words looked cold and clinical on the small phone screen. They were practical, necessary, and yet—the longer I stared at them—strangely ritualistic.

I leaned back and exhaled slowly, trying to center myself. Numbers, patterns, logic—those were still mine. The rest—Saraph, The Merge, fate—were variables to be mapped, mitigated, and contained.

Outside, the last of the tourist group dispersed, their laughter trailing off near the corner of Beacon and Joy as they made their way back downtown, some cutting through the quiet paths of the Boston Common. The tour guide's voice lingered behind them, offering thanks for their time and their tips before fading into the cold too. The city looked calm, composed, unaware.

Tonight, at Hotel Hawthorne, we'd meet again. It was another gathering, another renewal of purpose. I already knew what The Merge expected of me; there was nothing new to learn, only to remember and build upon.

Still, as I caught my reflection before heading out to meet my private helicopter, binder in hand, the thought lingered: was this free will, or just the comfort of doing what had always felt like a no-brainer because I had finally discovered it was worth the tradeoff?

QUESTIONS FOR PERSONAL REFLECTION

1. Jarvis's encounters with The Tuned (cult members) mirror many cult-recruitment techniques. Which ones did you notice? How were they portrayed? For example, where do you see love-bombing, the discouragement of outside contact, or the creation of an "us-versus-them" mindset?

2. Some of The Merge's (the cult) recruitment methods may feel familiar beyond a cult setting. Do you notice similar patterns in your everyday interactions? Think about your schools, workplaces, favorite sports teams, religious gatherings, or even where you shop.

3. Every Tuned (cult member) believes The Merge (the cult) will save them, even though only one will become the reincarnation of Saraph (the final goal of ascension). Why do you think so many still

joined? What does this reveal about hope and desperation? Do you see similar patterns in your everyday interactions?

4. The novel features many moments that seem supernatural. Do you think these events were truly supernatural, or could they be explained by psychological and physical factors, such as stress, illness, food poisoning, lack of sleep, or the characters' vulnerabilities and the influence of others?

5. Jarvis's academic background plays a large role in how he interprets events. How much do you think education protects someone from manipulation, and how much can it blind them?

6. Do you believe free will truly exists, or is it an illusion shaped by persuasion, personal vulnerabilities, and the appeal of certain benefits? How does the novel challenge or reinforce your view?

7. Do you think a group can behave in cult-like ways even if the larger organization itself isn't a cult? Where do you see that line being drawn?

8. Finally, if you have ever been part of a real-
   life cult, what led you to join, how did you
   first realize it was a cult, and what helped
   you finally leave?

GROUP DISCUSSION & ACTIVITIES

1. In small groups, choose one prompt from *Questions for Personal Reflection* and have everyone answer the same question. After sharing, invite each person to introduce what they do for work. Were you surprised by anyone's response? Did their answers seem connected to their personal experiences?

2. Repeat Activity 1, but invite each person to introduce their childhood upbringing instead of what they do for work.

3. Repeat Activity 1, but invite each person to introduce their religious beliefs instead of what they do for work.

FREE EBOOK

Review *The Merge* on any platform (Amazon, Goodreads, YouTube, etc.) and receive the next eBook in the series for free.

More information at https://www.jesseneo.com/free

ABOUT THE AUTHOR

JESSE NEO is an Australian-born second-generation immigrant and author of psychological fiction, and holds a PhD in Computer Science. He is an avid traveler, having spent extended periods in many major cities around the world, so much so that he often feels like a local in them. Many of these experiences have shaped the settings and atmospheres in his stories. Visit jesseneo.com.